I0623495

You Can't Delete You

Geneva Gordon

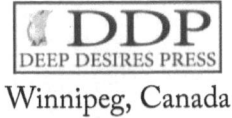

Winnipeg, Canada

Developmental editor: Brenda Clotildes
Proofreader: Francisco Feliciano

Published July 2023 by Deep Desires Press, an imprint of Story Perfect Inc.

Deep Desires Press
PO Box 51053 Tyndall Park
Winnipeg, Manitoba R2X 3B0
Canada

Visit http://www.deepdesirespress.com for more scorching hot erotica and erotic romance.

You Can't Delete You

CHAPTER ONE

Graham advanced and crouched behind a burned-out car. He stopped and listened. Hearing nothing, he poked his head out, surveying the street ahead. It was empty. In a crouch he ran for the next burned-out car. He listened for a second longer and peeked through the empty windows scanning the street ahead of him. Papers blew in the wind, skittering across the street. He brought his rifle up, looked through the scope, again scanning the surrounding buildings and cars for movement. Nothing. Another burned out wreck ahead.

Darting out from behind the car he ran for the next burned-out automobile. Halfway there a shot rang out, he was hit. He fell forward gracelessly and died on the spot.

"Who did that? Who shot me?" he yelled into his headset.

"Zing, man! It was me," a girl responded. "Sorry." She giggled.

Graham scanned the names of the players on the side of the screen.

"Who are you?" he asked.

"Guerillagurl," she responded, "which one are you?"

"Tapdat."

On the screen, his man stood. Graham's attention swung back to the screen. He had two more lives to go. He hadn't been past this point before, and he was excited to explore new territory. "I gotta go," he said.

"I'll go with you," Guerillagurl said.

"Okay," Tapdat said. "Just don't shoot me again!"

It didn't take him long to get back behind the burned-out car. He had been here before. This was his fifth attempt at trying to get past this point. He sprung out from behind the car, running to the next vehicle carcass. Guerillagurl appeared at his side. Together they crouched behind it.

"We gotta go into that building," Tapdat said.

"I know," Guerillagurl said.

"You ready?" Tapdat asked.

"Locked and loaded," she responded.

"Let's go," he said.

"Balls to the wall!" she shouted.

They stood and started running. They passed a hardware store, approaching an intersection. Suddenly a horde of zombies came storming out of the side street. They stood side by side mowing down zombies with their machine guns. A zombie came up behind them, grabbing Tapdat.

Tapdat, punched his controller again and again, trying to throw the zombie off. He broke free and attacked it using his machine gun as a club. In the meantime, Guerillagurl emptied her machine gun. She had to wait two seconds to reload. Two seconds would cost her her life.

"Tapdat!" she yelled. "I'm out!"

Tapdat stomped the zombie's head, killing it. He turned and unloaded on the dwindling zombies. The two seconds expired. It seemed like ten minutes. Guerillagurl reloaded and together they finished off the horde.

"That's what I said," Tapdat crowed.

"Yeah, eat lead," Guerillagurl added.

They played for another two hours advancing, killing zombies, dying, watching each other's backs. They chatted while planning their next moves, where to go and how to solve puzzles. They both loved video games, didn't mind school and had seen the latest blockbuster in the theatre. Another voice came over Tapdat's headset.

"Graham, dinner's ready."

"Just a minute, Mom," he said.

"Graham, your mother told you to come to the table," a male voice responded.

"Dad!"

"Never mind. Turn that thing off, dinner's ready."

"I gotta go," Tapdat said. "Maybe we can play later."

"Sure," Guerillagurl said.

Graham logged out. Guerillagurl, having lost her partner, logged out too. She would look for Tapdat next time she was online. He was kinda funny, and they played well together. She had homework to do anyway. She plugged in her controller to charge before she went to her desk and opened her backpack, pulling out her books.

Two days later Guerillagurl logged on, looking for a game. Scrolling through the levels and players, a message popped up on the screen:

Tapdat: That u?

Guerillagurl: Yeah, where u at?

Tapdat: Level 4. Sewer System. You comin?

Guerillagurl: On my way.

Guerillagurl found him quickly. They teamed up and worked their way through the sewer system. They reconnoitred, finding weapons, ammunition and medical supplies.

Ahead of them was a short ladder descending into a pool of water. A short distance away was another ladder leading out of the water up to a small platform and a door.

Tapdat: We gotta get to that door.

Guerillagurl: Yeah. It's been pretty quiet so far, I bet something big is coming.

Tapdat: Could be. We should see if there's more ammo.

Guerillagurl: Yeah. A machine gun would be nice.

Tapdat: Only if we find some ammo too.

Guerillagurl: Roger that.

They approached the ladder. Tapdat stepped down onto the first rung. The water beneath them started to boil with activity.

Tapdat: What the...

Guerillagurl: I got your six Tap.

Guerillagurl brought her gun into firing position. Tapdat stepped down another rung. The water churned faster.

Tapdat: I got a bad feeling about this.

Guerillagurl: Just go. Run as fast as you can when you hit the water.

Tapdat jumped off the rung, landing in the water. Rats

started popping out of the water, swimming toward him. Hundreds of rats. Tapdat started shooting. Guerillagirl landed with a splash beside him. She emptied her gun, grabbed another clip and slapped it in.

Guerillagurl: Run!

Tapdat ran, Guerillagurl hot on his heels. More rats popped out of the water ahead of them. Rats climbed their pants onto their backs, each bite decreasing their lives. Running and shooting they made it to the next ladder and quickly scaled it. On the landing, they shook themselves off, grabbing rats and throwing them back into the water. For good measure, they each drank a bottle of medicine, replenishing the life they lost from the rat attack.

Guerillagurl: If Mr. Whiskers were here this would NOT have happened.

Tapdat: That's hilarious. You have a cat named Mr. Whiskers? Hahahahahaha.

Guerillagurl: Laugh all you want, he's a killer. No rats in this house. Let me guess, your cat's name is Rambo.

Tapdat: We don't have a cat. Just old Cooper. He's a mutt.

In the game, Tapdat reached out and tried to open the door. It was locked.

Tapdat: Shit!

Guerillagurl: Try shooting the door!

Tapdat aimed at it and emptied his gun. The lock held.

Guerillagurl: Here, let me try.

Tapdat stood back. Guerillagurl came forward and kicked the door. She took out her gun and shot at the lock. She pulled on the handle. The door would not open.

Tapdat: Now what? There's no where else for us to go. We've checked all the other rooms.

Guerillagurl: Yeah. Do you think there's anything under the water?

Tapdat: Too shallow. It came up to our knees. We would have seen a hatch or something.

Guerillagurl: Okay. Let's look at the walls then.

They turned to face the way they had come. They scanned the walls. There were no other ladders. Nor were there any niches or handholds of any sort.

Tapdat: So that's a no.

Guerillagurl turned back toward the door.

Guerillagurl: Look over the door!

She jumped up in front of the door, grabbing onto the jamb. She put one hand up above the jamb, her view changed. Just out of sight and within reach was a rung.

Guerillagurl: There's another ladder up here.

Tapdat: Excellent!

They climbed the ladder, Guerillagurl first, followed by Tapdat. At the top was a storage room with some lockers and broken furniture. They split up, Tapdat heading for the lockers, Guerillagurl checking behind the furniture.

Tapdat: Gurl, your six!

Guerillagurl spun around. A zombie! She brought her gun up. Head shot! The zombie went down.

Guerillagurl: Thanks, Tap. Nothing here. You find anything?

Tapdat: Not yet.

Tapdat went to the last locker and opened it. It was empty. He walked past it into a beam of light that they hadn't noticed. Behind the row of lockers was a hole in the wall that they had been unable to see.

Tapdat: There's a hole in the wall. We've gotta move these lockers.

He leaned against the lockers and pushed. They didn't budge. Guerillagurl appeared at his side. Together they put their shoulders on the lockers and shoved. Metal scraped on the concrete floor as the lockers moved an inch. They pushed again—another scrape and again, another scrape. One more push and they could see through the hole. They could also hear the moaning of zombies.

Tapdat: You ready?

Guerillagurl: Locked and loaded.

Tapdat: Let's go.

Guerillagurl: Balls to the wall.

And that is how it started, two twelve-year olds on opposite sides of the country, gaming their way into a friendship and a tight zombie-killing machine.

CHAPTER TWO

Two years later, Guerillagurl raced along a mountain track in a Ferrari. The clock was ticking. She was headed for first place. A Lamborghini appeared out of nowhere, nipping at her rear fender. She swerved to block him.

"No fair," Tapdat said.

"All's fair in gaming bro," Guerillagurl said, laughing.

Tapdat, squeezed by on her right. She gritted her teeth, "I don't think so, Tap."

Concentrating, they lapsed into silence. There was a hairpin turn coming up and then the finish line. Tapdat didn't brake soon enough. He spun out on the shoulder. Guerillagurl breezed past, making the corner and crossing the finish line.

"Good job, Gurl," he said.

"Yeah, I rule. Where've you been? Haven't seen you for a couple of days."

"Been doing hard time in detention," he said.

"Detention? What did you do?" This was nothing new since his dad left a couple of months ago. Tapdat was such a nice guy, her best friend. She couldn't understand why he was always getting in trouble. He didn't seem to understand it either when she asked him why.

"Nothing."

"Yeah, they put kids in detention at my school for doing nothing too. What did you do?"

"I don't want to talk about it." On his end, Tapdat couldn't understand why Gurl was his friend. She was one of those "good girls". In real life she wouldn't even look at him, much less speak to him. He treasured her friendship.

"C'mon Tap." Persistence usually paid off for Gurl. If she kept nagging him, he would more than likely tell her what she wanted to know.

"Really, I don't want to talk about it."

"Well I do. Another fight?"

"No."

"Skipping class again?"

"No."

"Hogging the ball in gym?"

"Hogging the ball! What are you talking about?" He smiled. Like he would get detention for hogging the ball! Gurl made him laugh.

She heard the smile in his voice. One more push and Tap would crack. "Just tell me already or I'm going to keep guessing."

"Maybe I was 'disruptive' in class."

"Like talking?"

"Yeah, like talking... back to the teacher, and 'talking' really loud."

"Yelling? You were yelling at the teacher?" This was beyond Gurl's understanding. To her, teachers were authority figures, and definitely not to be yelled at.

"I told you I didn't want to talk about it, and I meant

it, Gurl. It's not like I don't have any homework." He threatened to end the game and their chat.

"Okay, okay. Wanna go again?" Gurl knew when to push and when to back off. If this was really serious, Tap would eventually circle around to it, and they would talk about it. Maybe not even today.

"You ready to lose this time?"

"Says who?"

"The mighty Tapdat, that's who. You ready?"

"Locked and loaded."

"Let's go."

"Balls to the wall."

Time flew by as they competed against each other in a private room. They decided to move to another course. As the game segued to the new track, Carly said, "Hey, I am starting to spend more time with Brittany and Melissa."

"Who?"

"I told you about them before. We're in homeroom this year. I ran into them in the mall a couple of weeks ago and we have been hanging out since then."

"Great. What are they like?"

"Probably not your idea of fun. We try different make up and talk about boys and clothes and stuff."

"You are right about that, Gurl, not my idea of fun. But if you like them I'm sure that I would like them too."

"Carly, turn that off. It's time for bed." Her mother stood in her bedroom door.

"Mom, just a couple more minutes. It's Tap and I haven't spoken to him for a couple of days," Guerillagurl pleaded.

"Another 30 minutes, that's all." She relented, smiling.

"You rock," Guerillagurl said to her mother. "You heard that right," she asked Tapdat. "I gotta sign off in half an hour."

"Yeah," he said. "Hey, wanna give me your email address?" he asked hesitantly.

"Uh, why?"

"Look, my time's running out. My card expires in a couple of days. Money's real tight now that my dad's gone and my mom can't afford to buy more minutes," he explained. "I kinda thought, maybe we could, you know, email and stuff."

Guerillagurl was shocked by the news, shocked that she could possibly lose a good friend. They spent so much time trash talking, joking and just chatting about things. She didn't hesitate. "You got a pen?"

"No, can't afford one. I'll just slice my finger and write it in blood," he said seriously.

"Uh…"

"C'mon! Of course, I got a pen."

She gave him her email address. She got her first email from Tapdat the next day:

Tapdat: Hey is this you? Just checking. Want to make sure I have the right addy. Mail me back.

She responded immediately:

Guerillagurl: Who is this and where did you get my address? Hahahahaha. Yes, it's me. Hope you're staying out of trouble. It's only been a day since we spoke so I will assume you are good.

She hit the send button. A second later a chat box appeared on her screen.

Tapdat: You're on.

Guerillagurl: Yes. You got my email?

Tapdat: Yeah. What you doing?

Guerillagurl: Homework. Ugh. Got to think up an experiment for science, do it, and then write it up. What are you doing?

Tapdat: I should be doing homework too but am thinking of heading out with my guys.

Guerillagurl: You should do your homework first Tap. Do you have a lot?

Tapdat: No.

Guerillagurl: Then why not do it. Shock and amaze your teachers. They'll never believe that you actually did your homework.

Tapdat: There's a thought. Annoyance by homework.

Guerillagurl: Yeah. Make them pass you. Do your homework. Study for tests. They'll be sorry they ever sent you to detention.

Tapdat: Careful Gurl, you're bordering on a motivational email.

Guerillagurl: OMG. Tap if you fail to plan, then you plan to fail. Anything is possible. Dream big. Stop me, please.

Tapdat: LOL. You make me laugh.

Guerillagurl: Always there for you Tap. I gotta go, dinner's ready and my homework hasn't done itself yet— damn homework!

Tapdat: K.

Guerillagurl: Mail me later alligator.

Guerillagurl: OMG Tap, Joe asked me out!

Tapdat: That guy you think is cute?

Guerillagurl: Not cute! Dreamy! He's taking me to a movie on Friday.

Tapdat: You know he's only after one thing, don't you?

Guerillagurl: My superior intellect? Do you think he's a zombie after my brains? Ahhhhhh.

Tapdat: No, guess again.

Guerillagurl: My flair for fashion? I am more than willing to undress, er dress him.

Tapdat: You are so bad. I never thought of you as a bad Gurl. But, no, guess again.

Guerillagurl: My superb makeup application techniques?

Tapdat: No, guess again.

Guerillagurl: I don't get that vibe from him Tap. I think he's really nice. Besides, I'm not ready for that yet.

Tapdat: That's my Gurl. What do your friends think about him? What are their names again?

Guerillagurl: Melissa and Brittany. They think he's okay. Brittany has history with him. She says he seems nice. Enough with my love life Tap. Tell me about Sammi. You still seeing her?

Tapdat: I'm seeing a lot of her—hahaha.

Guerillagurl: Really Tap, and you're on me about Joe.

Tapdat: You're my best friend Gurl, I'm just trying to save you some heartache.

Guerillagurl: I appreciate that Tap but I gotta live my life and you gotta use birth control.

Tapdat: Yeah, yeah. I'm being careful. I'm not ready to be a daddy.

Guerillagurl: Glad to hear it. Wow, look at the time! I gotta go. I'm meeting my besties at the mall in half an hour.

Tapdat: Okay. Say hi to Melissa and Brittany for me.

Guerillagurl: Will do. They will say hi back.

Carly logged off, did a quick refresh of her makeup and ran out the door. She hopped in the car and drove to the mall to meet Melissa and Brittany. They met in the food court and talked over French fries and sodas. They were as excited about Carly's date as Carly was. She told them what Tap said and they agreed that that was a possibility and then offered up advice on what to do if Joe made any moves on her. Their suggestions got more and more bizarre. They ended up laughing over the whole thing.

Her date with Joe turned out to be a disaster.

Guerillagurl: Ugh, he kept trying to feel me up. It was so gross.

Tapdat: Don't want to say I told you so, but I told you so.

Guerillagurl: Yeah, I know. One good thing is I don't have any classes with him so I don't have to see him everyday. I know it's stupid but I thought he was going to be my future.

Tapdat: We're too young to be settling down Gurl. There is someone more special than Joe in your future because you deserve it.

Guerillagurl: Thanks Tap. So what's new with you?

Tapdat: Got arrested on Saturday.

Guerillagurl: WHAT!

Tapdat: Don't yell. My mom has been doing enough of that.

Guerillagurl: What happened? Why were you arrested?

Tapdat: I went cruising with some friends. We stopped to get gas and one of my buds started an argument with some guy in another car. They started fighting. The other guy had some friends with him. and when they ganged up on my buddy, I jumped in to help. Someone called the cops and it turned out the car we were in was stolen.

Guerillagurl: Did you know that?

Tapdat: Might have had a clue.

Guerillagurl: And a fight. Are you okay?

Tapdat: Of course, I'm okay. Not a scratch on me.

Guerillagurl: So what's going to happen now.

Tapdat: Not sure. Gotta see a lawyer. Mom's pissed. We can't afford a lawyer so we have to use Legal Aid and she doesn't have a lot of faith in them.

Guerillagurl: You're not going to end up in jail are you?

Tapdat: Hope not.

Guerillagurl: I hope not too. You gotta find new friends Tap.

Tapdat: I know.

Guerillagurl: I'm serious Tap.

Tapdat: I know Gurl. It doesn't matter anyway, I'm grounded forever according to my mom.

Carly came home from school, went into the kitchen, got a juice from the fridge and opened her laptop on the marble island. She logged on and immediately checked her email. Still nothing from Tap. It'd been almost a week and that was a long time for them. For the first time she wondered if she should be worried.

She was saddened and disappointed in Tap. When he was first arrested a year and a half ago, she thought that that would have encouraged him to turn his life around, but it hadn't. He still hung out with the same crowd, and he had been arrested more times than she cared to remember.

She pulled up his last email and reread it. More trouble, of course, a new girl, also of course, something about a new program he was going to have to take part in as a condition of his parole, the usual references to Star Trek (he was such a geek), and, as usual his comments on her life.

She shut down Outlook and pulled up her history essay. If she finished this in the next two hours, she would have time to meet Melissa and Brittany at the mall for a bit.

Guerillagurl—Katherine her full name in real life and just Carly for short—had turned into a beauty. She had been gangly and underdeveloped as a teen. She had grown into an attractive girl. At 18 she was stunning. Shoulder length auburn hair, brown eyes, plump lips, all on top of a slim athletic body, which she attributed to good genes because if she was anything, it was not athletic.

Her dad walked into the kitchen. He grabbed a water from the fridge. "That Tap?" he asked. "You should be doing your homework, Carly."

"I am doing my homework. Tap hasn't mailed me for a week." Did her voice just crack?

Her dad looked at her.

"It's just we always mail, all the time. It's been a week, Dad. I don't know if I should be worried."

He put a hand on her shoulder. "I don't think you should worry Carly. He's a young guy. He's probably just too busy with things."

"I know Dad, but he's my best friend."

"I thought Brittany and Melissa were your best friends."

"They are Dad, but Tap knows me better than anyone. I hope nothing happened to him."

"Well, I guess he could be in jail... again. Lord knows if he was physically in your life there was no way I would allow this friendship. That being said, there are a thousand reasons why he hasn't emailed you, a thousand good reasons. Don't worry pumpkin. You'll hear from him soon enough."

"I know. It's just that it's so unusual."

He kissed her forehead. "He'll email, you'll see."

Carly did finish her essay in time to go to the mall. She met Brittany and Melissa. They sat in the food court with an order of fries and colas. It wasn't long before they were joined by more friends. Carly managed to push thoughts of Tap out of her mind while she enjoyed being young and popular.

She came home and ran up the stairs to her bedroom. Shutting the door behind her, she pulled her phone out of her purse, fell on her bed, and checked her emails. Still nothing from Tap. She opened a new message.

Guerillagurl: Where u at? Haven't heard from you for a while. Everything ok?

She hoped that that would get a response.

Graduation was looming. The next few days were spent dress shopping, party planning and spending time with Melissa and Brittany. Despite all the activity Carly checked her emails at every opportunity. Still no mail from Tap. It was official, she was worried.

That night, homework and bedtime routine done, she lay in bed and turned off the light. Her thoughts turned to Tap. Where was he? What was he doing? Why wasn't he mailing her? Her phone dinged. Carly reached for it. She sat up and turned on her bedside lamp. A little envelope was in the Outlook icon.

"Be Tap, be Tap," she said as she opened the screen. There was an email, but not from Tap. It was an addy she didn't recognize. The re line though, that got her attention. *It's Tap*. She clicked on it immediately and opened the mail.

Tapdat: Hey Gurl, been in lock down in this new program. Straight from Court to here so, sorry, no time to let you know what happened. NO PHONE either! Confiscated immediately. No internet access either. Gotta earn it. Guess what? I been a good boy : c) S'up?

Relief flooded her body as she read on. It was an experimental behaviour modification thing. He was out in the country somewhere. No internet, no TV, no phone, nowhere to go, nothing to do. There were boys and girls, separate dorms though. They spent days in intensive group therapy sessions. The "experimental" part of the therapy was acting. They were studying drama, doing acting exercises, tapping into their emotions. Tap liked it. Thought some of it was tough, but fun.

Tapdat: I think this could be something new for me Gurl. I'm kinda tired of who I am and where I'm going.

You still seeing that doofus Terry? You and the girls staying out of trouble? Hey, if you get arrested maybe you'll end up in here with me. We can finally meet. That'd be okay.

Anyway, time's running out—of course I only have half an hour. I'm gonna be here for another three weeks—ugh—so I'm not going to be mailing as much, but will when I can. Oh yeah, all incoming mails are read so, no sexy stuff, K. LOL, as if.

Phasers on stun Gurl. Mail ya later.

Carly didn't hesitate, she opened a new message and started typing. She congratulated him on his good behaviour and told him she thought that it was really cool that he was acting. Then she went into her life, yes, she and the girls were staying out of trouble; Terry wasn't a doofus, by the way; graduation was next week. She ended, as she always did.

Locked and loaded. Balls to the wall.

CHAPTER THREE

Carly was studying for finals. This was her last year in university, majoring in journalism. She was confident that she would do well, she had certainly put in the work! It was a late night for her. She was watching the clock. 11:57. Okay, close enough. She closed her books, shut down her computer, got into bed and turned on the TV. It was already on the science fiction channel.

The crew was on an alien planet. They had to find food. Suddenly they were surrounded by aliens. Chief Officer Scott stepped forward, his hands out.

"We mean no harm."

One of the aliens shot him.

Cut to the opening montage.

Chief Officer Scott was Tap. He wasn't the star of the show, but he had a significant part. Carly watched every show, even the reruns. It was pretty much a schlocky sci fi show, cheap sets, next to no special effects and on late at night. This was their second season, rumoured to be their last. Tap was bummed about it, but he was hopeful. His agent was working hard at getting him something else as soon as possible.

Carly was hopeful as well. She wanted the best for Tap. That experimental program had turned his life around. He had dropped his old friends when he got out and moved to

New York. He had spent his days auditioning and waiting on tables, the cliched existence of a struggling actor. He started out with a few commercials, finally got a bit part in a Broadway play, then guest spots on TV dramas, finally this show.

Tap was a double threat—talented and good looking. He had developed into a man. He was tall with a body that was every woman's dream thanks to hours spent at the gym. He had beautiful green eyes, longish dark blond hair rakishly pushed back off his face and full, kissable lips. For a budget-friendly late-night sci fi show, female viewers were through the roof. No wonder.

Not surprisingly Chief Officer Scot hadn't been killed, merely stunned. Food was located, they escaped the aliens and would be back next week with another episode.

Carly texted Tap:

Guerillagurl: Great show. Glad you lived. What's next?

Tapdat: You know that's a secret. What I can tell you is that I live.

Guerillagurl: Spoiler alert! Guess I don't need to watch next week.

Tapdat: That would be devastating. I need every viewer I can get.

Guerillagurl: Okay, then. What's the name of the show again? I don't want to miss it.

Tapdat: LOL. The Chief Officer Scott show : c)

Guerillagurl: Oh yeah, right. What part do you play again?

Tapdat: You're killing me Gurl.

Guerillagurl: Were those sparks flying between you and the alien soldier?

Tapdat: You know I never kiss and tell.

Guerillagurl: Right. Now who's kidding who. Let me guess, you Tapdat!

Tapdat: Maybe. But if I had to give a definitive answer to your probing question I would have to say Hells yes. Hey, how's studying going? Did you hear anything about that internship at *Eyes on You* that you applied for?

Guerillagurl: I'm gonna ace finals. I'm pretty sure about that. Haven't heard about the internship. I'm not worried though. Parents say I can take some time off after grad. Don't want to tho. Excited to start living my live, ya know.

Tapdat: I hear you Gurl. Time off would be nice tho. Hey, why don't you come to New York? We can finally meet. I'll show you around. You can come to the set, watch a taping.

Guerillagurl: Really? I can come and spend a whole day watching you work while I sit there unemployed? How can I say this? Hmmm, let me see, no.

Tapdat: Come on. It's not all work. We can go clubbing, out to eat, go to.... wait for it, Comic Con. William Shatner is going to be there!

Guerillagurl: OMG! Then what? We'll have to find out where he's staying. Then we can go stand outside his hotel to see if we can meet him. Then we can get arrested for stalking. But wait, are you going to be wearing your Captain Kirk uniform?

Tapdat: Maybe.

Guerillagurl: GEEK!

Tapdat: Millions of women would disagree with you.

Guerillagurl: Millions of women who don't know you as well as I do.

Tapdat: You're trying to distract me. Why don't you come? I'll pay for your flight.

Guerillagurl: Yeah, no. Thanks anyway. You gotta hang onto that cash. What if you get cancelled?

Tapdat: You gotta live in the moment Gurl. Tomorrow doesn't exist. Now is all that matters. It's almost like you don't want to meet.

That made her pause momentarily. She did and she didn't want to meet Tap. Sure, it was easy to be his friend over the phone and internet. Maybe he was different in real life. Maybe she wouldn't like him.

Guerillagurl: Yikes. That's some deep shit, Tap. I'm gonna take a few days to try to digest that. It's late. I've got a 9 a.m. exam. I gotta go.

Tapdat: You ready?

Guerillagurl: Locked and loaded.

Tapdat: Let's go.

Guerillagurl: Balls to the wall.

Tapdat: That's my Gurl. Sweet dreams.

Guerillagurl: You too Chief Officer Scott. Mail ya later.

Carly turned off the lights and drifted off to sleep thinking of Tapdat. It was funny. He was her best friend but had never seen her. She didn't think he knew her real name. He always called her Gurl.

She knew everything about him though, not just his stats—she knew what he looked like, she knew his past, she knew his present and she knew his personality. He was a great guy. She felt lucky to be his friend. She thought, and hoped, that he felt the same way about her.

CHAPTER FOUR

In the end Carly aced her finals, as she expected; she got that internship, which was a surprise; and she moved to Los Angeles. She had studied journalism and her internship was with a national entertainment news show, *Eyes on You.* That catapulted her into a whole new sphere of people: entertainers, reporters, paparazzi, writers, actors, sycophants. She began as a junior assistant in the research department. She was hired on after her internship was over. She wrote interview questions for the hosts.

Dan, the producer of the show came to her desk. "Katherine, we've got a situation."

"Yeah," Carly responded. She was thinking: a situation? What does that mean? Am I fired?

"Tonya is in Cannes and Tim Carter is only available for an interview today," Dan said. "Jerry is covering the Celebrity Charity Baseball Event. There's no one to do the interview and Tim is going to be in the studio in 45 minutes."

"Okay…" Carly said.

"You're going to do it," Dan said. It wasn't a question.

"Me? But I've never done an interview. I've never been on TV," Carly stated the obvious facts.

"Doesn't matter. You did the research. You wrote the questions, right?" He looked at her.

"Yes, but…"

"No buts, we've got"—he looked at his watch—"forty minutes now. Get to make up. They'll fix your hair."

Carly put her hand on her hair.

"Someone will bring you something to wear," he added.

Carly looked down at her outfit—tank top and shorts. "But…"

"What did I say? No buts. Go!"

Carly stood.

"Now," Dan ordered.

Carly picked up the questions she had prepared and ran to make up. She was going to interview Tim Carter. Tim Carter, one of the hottest hunks in Hollywood. This was a dream come true and a nightmare at the same time. A dream come true because Tim Carter had been her crush since her teens and a nightmare because she was going to go off script. A move that, she realized, could end her career just as it was getting started.

Twenty-five minutes later her hair was done, her make up applied. She had been given a short black jacket to wear over her tank top. She was sitting in a director's chair in the studio while the crew did a light and sound check. Someone ran up with another director's chair and sat it across from her.

Twenty minutes later Tim Carter walked in and sat down, facing her. He gave her a killer smile and a wink. "Hi," he said.

Carly gulped. "Hi." She reached out and they shook hands. Another technician ran up with a bottle of water for Tim.

Suddenly someone shouted, "Quiet on set!"

All noise stopped. The countdown started. "Rolling in five, four, three, two."

"Tim," she started, "it's a pleasure to meet you."

"It's great to be here, Katherine." He smiled at the camera.

"So, tell me about your new film, *Common Ground*."

"Well, we shot it about a year ago in Georgia. It's a love story about a confederate soldier who is injured in the Civil War. He's found by a young widow who takes him in and cares for him while he recovers from his injuries. They fall in love. The South loses the war, of course, and we follow the couple as they deal with their new reality."

Carly held her question cards in a death grip. She swallowed, looked up at Tim and said, "There have been rumors circulating online about your relationship with Mandy Bevins. Would you care to comment?"

Sitting across from him, Carly saw Tim pause, look at his manager, and gulp. "You can't believe everything that you read on the internet, Katherine, but yes, I do know Mandy, she worked for me for a number of years. Unfortunately, we did not part on the best of terms and now she is carrying on a vendetta against me."

"She has some very serious allegations against you. She has accused you of stalking her, enlisting other employees to spy on her and sexual harassment and sexual assault."

"I know. Unbelievable, isn't it? I have offered to get her some help. I do wish only the best for her. As I said, she worked for me for five years." He shot Carly a look that told her to stop this line of questioning.

Carly took a deep breath, trying to steady her nerves. "If that were the case, Tim, those would certainly be noble actions on your part, but there have been others haven't there?"

"Others? What are you talking about."

"Other women. Other employees and associates who have also filed claims against you for the same thing, stalking, sexual harassment, assault…"

Tim glared at Katherine. "No comment. My lawyer will be in touch," he said as he stood, unhooked his microphone and walked out of the studio, his manager hot on his heels.

"Cut," the director said.

Carly stood, removed her mic and ran to the ladies' room, where she promptly threw up.

"What the hell, Katherine!" Dan yelled at her. "We don't do investigative journalism. We do feel good stories about celebrities. How many stars are going to be lining up to be interviewed by us now?"

"If they have nothing to hide, it shouldn't matter. Dan, the man is a danger to women, for God's sake."

"He was here to talk about his movie. This was a press junket. Not a fan girl crush ambush."

"People deserve to know about him. People need to know who their idols are. They need to know if these people are worthy of their adoration."

"You better hang on to your notes and documents.

We're going to be looking at a lawsuit because of you. Goddamn it, Katherine!"

"I stand by my research, Dan. It's true, all of it."

"I hope you're right. Now I've got to meet with the Network head. I don't know what else to say to you, but be prepared for the worst. I can't shield you from the consequences of this."

Carly returned to her desk. The day was almost over. She was pretty sure she would be out of a job by the time Dan was finished his meeting. She decided to leave early. They couldn't fire her if they couldn't find her—until tomorrow at least.

On the way home she stopped at a donut shop and picked up a dozen vanilla dipped with sprinkles. She entered her apartment, put the box of the ten remaining donuts on the living room table and went to change into her pajama shorts with the loose waist—she was going to need it. Coming back, she sat on the couch, pulled up Tap's cell number and texted him.

Guerillagurl: Hey, you there?

Waiting for a response she grabbed another donut. Looking out her windows, eating her donut, she held her phone in her hand waiting to hear from Tap. Five minutes later:

Tapdat: Yeah. Just got back from the gym. What you doing?

Guerillagurl: Nothing. Eating a donut.

Tapdat: Vanilla dipped?

Guerillagurl: Maybe.

Tapdat: With sprinkles?

Guerillagurl: Yeah.

Tapdat: What's wrong?

Guerillagurl: Bad day at work. Probably my last day too.

Tapdat: No.

Guerillagurl: Super yes.

Tapdat: Tell me.

Guerillagurl: I don't have to tell you. Just watch the show tonight.

Tapdat: Sending you a big hug Gurl. Maybe it's not as bad as you think.

Guerillagurl: Yeah, it's not as bad as I think. It's worse. I need another donut.

Tapdat: Donuts don't solve anything.

Guerillagurl: Yes they do. I'm gonna have another five at least!

Tapdat: While you're o.d.ing on sugar I'm gonna take a shower and watch the show. Text ya afterward. K.

Guerillagurl: KKKKKKKKK. Shit, the icing is makkkking the kkkkeys stickkkk.

Tapdat: Serves you right hahaha.

Guerillagurl: Shut up!

She couldn't help herself. 6:00 came and she turned on the show. Would they even air the interview? Would it be as bad as she imagined it would be?

The show opened with the usual fluff, Tonya in Cannes, covering the red carpet. Jerry at the Celebrity charity baseball game, some kid in North Dakota who had a viral video of her singing and dancing. Commercial. The interview.

Carly watched it while holding a pillow in her lap, ready to cover her face. Hey, she didn't look too bad on camera. She held her breath as the interview went from bad to worse. Tim got up and left the interview. Carly exhaled. Yeah, it was as bad as she thought it would be. She turned off the TV.

Her phone dinged. Tap was on.

Tapdat: Holy shit! Who is that Katherine Parsons chick?

Guerillagurl: My boss.

Tapdat: What a bitch. Is she like that in person?

Guerillagurl: She's not that bad. She's actually kinda nice. You would probably like her.

Tapdat: Doubtful. Man, she skewered Tim.

Guerillagurl: She thought people needed to know who he really was.

Tapdat: She probably just destroyed his career. He's gonna be selling cars in Atlanta within two years I'll bet. LOL. But hey, just because she gets fired doesn't mean you have to lose your job too.

Guerillagurl: I'm her personal assistant. If she goes, I go.

Tapdat: Let's just hope that doesn't happen then.

Guerillagurl: I'll be going into work tomorrow to pack up my desk.

Tapdat: Hey, why don't you come to New York. We can hang out.

Guerillagurl: Nah, I gotta start looking for another job. I gotta punch up my resume. I can only afford one more month's rent with what I have in savings.

Tapdat: You never say yes. Trip's on me, you won't have to pay for anything buddy.

Guerillagurl: Thanks again, Tap. Really. Why don't I get back to you on that. I've gotta go to work tomorrow to get fired officially. And I don't feel real good right now.

Tapdat: It won't be that bad.

Guerillagurl: No, I mean I don't feel good right now. My stomach is acting up.

Tapdat: Donuts.

Gueillagurl: Maybe.

Tapdat: Maybe? How many did you eat?

Guerillagurl: A couple.

Tapdat: How many, Gurl?

Guerillagurl: A few.

Tapdat: A few means two. ONLY two?

Guerillagurl: OKAY! 6 are you happy now?

Tapdat: OMG Gurl.

Guerillagurl: Shut up. I gotta go puke.

CHAPTER FIVE

The next day Carly slunk into work. It was probably just her imagination, but she felt that everyone was looking at her, even the cleaning lady!

Five minutes after sitting at her desk she got the call to Dan's office. This is it, she thought, so long career.

She walked to Dan's office. Was everyone avoiding her gaze?

"Just go in," his secretary said when she arrived.

She entered. Dan was sitting behind his desk on the phone. He pointed at the chairs.

"Yeah, she just walked in. Okay. I'll let you know." He hung up the phone, sat forward, clasping his hands on top of his desk. "Katherine," he began.

"I know I'm fired," Carly said meekly.

"You're right. In a sense," he said.

"So, what's the protocol?" Carly asked. "Two weeks pay? Turn in my id? Escort to the front door with my box of personal belongings?"

"We decided to go in a different direction with you, Katherine," he said. "Head office has decided to offer you a raise and a spot on a new show. They have a news magazine show in development. Something more serious, not just actors. They've been looking to sign some TV news journalists. They liked what they saw in the Tim Carter interview."

Carly was trying to process this. Was she hearing what she thought she was?

"Wait," she held up her hand. "Are you saying I still have a job?"

"Only if you're interested. I'm sorry to say we can't keep you on here. The type of interview you did with Tim doesn't fit our format. But, there is a spot for you on *Informed* if you want it. An on-camera spot. No more behind the scenes for you. You'll be the entertainment reporter, doing in-depth celebrity interviews. What do you say?"

"What do I say? I say hell yes."

Carly packed her desk and took her box of personal items to the sixth floor where she was introduced to her new coworkers and taken to her office—yes, office! The rest of the day she met with the executives who explained to her what they wanted to see on the show, what they wanted to see from her, what her new schedule would be.

At the end of the day, she got on the elevator to go home. It stopped on the second floor, her old office. Paul Stevens walked on. He was an up-and-coming director and a friend. The studios were keeping an eye on him. It was rumoured that he had just been given a script that could take him from a good director to a great director. He had been on her old show for a quick interview.

"Carly," he exclaimed as he walked on.

"Paul, great to see you," she responded.

"Heard that there are great things happening for you," he said.

"Likewise, Paul. It's a great day isn't it," Carly responded.

"Yeah, pretty good. Hey, let's go for a drink, I haven't seen you for a while. You can fill me in on your new job."

"Love to. How about Amaro's, it's just around the corner."

"Okay, see you in fifteen."

Paul and Carly sat across from each other in Amaro's nursing their drinks and sharing a plate of nachos.

"So, I get assignments and get to work my own stories too. It's the best of both worlds. I'm excited about it," Carly told Paul.

"That's great. Being in 'the business' I guess you've heard about the script."

"Yes, I have. An epic romance. Lots of studios were fighting for that script and you got picked to direct it. That's exciting. So what's the timeline?"

"I'm going to New York in a couple of weeks to work with the writer, finetune the script. A lot of pre-production work has been done so we hope to have it cast in the next two months and then start shooting in three months. It should be in theatres this time next year."

"So you're going to be gone for over a year?"

"No, I'll be back in town to edit but I will be gone for maybe up to six months."

"That's a long time. Do you have anyone in mind for any of the roles?"

"Not yet. We've been approached by a couple of actors wanting the roles but I've got some people in mind that I want to audition."

"Anyone I know?"

"Probably not. There's an actor I want to try. He's doing some late-night sci-fi show. If he's interested and can free up the time I think he might just be perfect."

Carly's ears perked up. Did he mean Tap? An actor on a late-night sci-fi show? How many other actors could there be? Probably more than she knew about.

"You don't mean Chief Officer Scott do you? What's that guy's name? I can't remember."

"I'm not mentioning any names." Paul smiled and winked at her.

"I'm a fan. I would go to see the movie just to see him."

"He has incredible numbers in female viewers. There are probably thousands of women like you who would go just to see him. It certainly can't hurt the box office."

At that point Carly wanted to jump up and run home to email Tap. But she had to play this cool. If she thought it would help Tap get the part, she would have told Paul that she knew Gray North but, then again, maybe it would hurt his chances if Paul knew they were acquainted. Better to keep it to herself.

"So when are you going to New York? We should get together with the gang before then."

"Three weeks from now I'll be in the Big Apple. A night out before I leave would be great."

That turned the conversation to mutual friends and lead to another drink before they parted ways.

Carly texted Tap as soon as she came home.

Guerillagurl: You home? Say yes.

Tapdat: Yes. What do you want me to say next?

Guerillagurl: What are you doing?

Tapdat: Getting ready to meet some friends. Got some bad news today and my buddies are going to try to cheer me up.

Guerillagurl: What bad news?

Tapdat: We were cancelled. Got the notification today.

Guerillagurl: Tap, I'm so sorry to hear that. I'd give you a big hug if I were there.

Tapdat: Thanks Gurl. I'm hoping I'll be able to get another show right away. My numbers weren't bad as Chief Officer Scott. That's a big help for me.

Guerillagurl: That's true. But, hey, don't be too quick to jump into another show. There might be something bigger coming your way.

Tapdat: That'd be nice.

Guerillagurl: Something bigger, like a movie.

Tapdat: I could handle that.

Guerillagurl: So maybe wait a while, like, maybe, three weeks, before you start sending out resumes.

Tapdat: Why three weeks? Are you trying to tell me something Gurl? Three weeks is pretty specific.

Guerillagurl: Maybe I've heard something.

Tapdat: Really? What have you heard?

Guerillagurl: I can't tell you anything right now Tap but I'm working on getting more intel. You know I've got your six.

Tapdat: You always do. What happened with your job? You don't seem upset.

Guerillagurl: Oh yeah. Guess who has a new job on a new program?

Tapdat: No way! A new program? Right on. I knew they wouldn't fire you. When do you start?

Guerillagurl: Already did. I'm going to be doing in-depth interviews with celebrities.

Tapdat: If the Tim Carter interview is an example of what you'll be doing you'll be great. Hey, just got a text from one of my pals. I gotta go hook up with them.

Guerillagurl: Sure. Have fun Tap.

Tapdat: You ready?

Guerillagurl: Locked and loaded.

Tapdat: Let's go.

Guerillagurl: Balls to the wall.

Three weeks later Carly texted Tap: Don't ask why, just be sure you are at Shots and Drafts on Saturday afternoon. Paul Stevens will be there. If you don't know who he is Google him. You need to talk to him.

CHAPTER SIX

Over the next six months Carly earned her own celebrity status as the interviewer of celebrities. She was feared and loved by them. She could destroy careers. She could endear misunderstood or vilified personalities. She could enhance profiles. And she did it all with solid research. Lawsuits had been threatened and quashed with facts that could not be refuted.

Paul Stevens had directed his movie, an epic romance, *The Thunder Roared.* He was back in town editing, involved in post-production. The buzz about his movie was good. It would be released in another couple of months and was one of the most anticipated releases of the year.

Tap had gone to Shots and Drafts on that Saturday. He met Paul Stevens, who was confused about why Tap was there and didn't know who Gurl was. But Paul had a couple of hours to kill and, since he was a fan of Chief Officer Scott and his show, they spent some time talking. Paul told Tap he should audition for the male lead for this new movie he was working on. Tap aced the audition and got the part.

The movie opened with great reviews. Tap was "discovered" as the hottest leading man in a generation. He was in every magazine, on every morning talk show, the new face for a top fashion house. Tap was Gray North and Gray North was her next interview.

Guerillagurl: S'up Tap.

Tapdat: Just having a soda.

Guerillagurl: What? Sugar water going into that temple you call a body?

Tapdat: One won't kill me.

Guerillagurl: True. The last time you had a soda was when you broke up with What's 'Er Name.

Tapdat: Nicole, for the hundredth time.

Guerillagurl: So, what's wrong Tap?

Tapdat: Why should anything be wrong?

Guerillagurl: Cuz you having a soda is like me eating a dozen vanilla dipped donuts. It's a sign, Tap.

Tapdat: Okay. So, my career may be ending in the very near future. You still have an extra bedroom? I might need a place to stay.

Guerillagurl: What? What happened?

Tapdat: Nothing yet.

Guerillagurl: Am I going to have to drag it out of you? Just tell me.

Tapdat: My agent scheduled an interview with Katherine Parsons.

Guerillagurl: LOL. I know. I just found out about it. I have to do research on you Tap. Is there absolutely anything about you that I don't know? I know, let's rehash your 7th grade relationship with Tonya. To this day I still don't know what you saw in her. You know I hated her.

Tapdat: Sure, laugh at me. Your boss is a ball buster and she'll rake me over the coals about Tonya. You know the only reason I still remember her is because you hated her so much! Hey! Are you going to be there? Maybe we can finally meet. We can finally hang out.

Guerillagurl: I won't be there and if I was, I would be the one that you wouldn't notice anyway. If you move to L.A., sure, we can hang. But you're going to be busy doing movie star stuff. I'll still be working nine to five.

They chatted for hours that seemed like minutes. They always gossiped about their friends and families, their jobs and people they knew. They always ended their chats the same way:

Tapdat: Ready?

Guerillagurl: Locked and loaded.

Tapdat: Let's go.

Guerillagurl: Balls to the wall.

Two weeks later Gray was sitting in the studio, in the director's chair that had seen the end of careers. He was dressed in jeans, a white tee and a leather jacket. He was leaning forward with his hands clasped. His leg was furiously pumping up and down.

The studio door opened. Katherine Parsons walked in. She sat across from him, arranging her notes on her lap. The sound girl walked up and clipped a mic to the neckline of her dress.

Gray had seen Katherine on TV. Who hadn't? In person she was breathtaking. She was tall, slim, had breasts that he would like to see up close and personal. Her face was flawless. Her skin was smooth, her brown eyes seemed to be shining with humour (oh no), her brown hair hung just past her shoulders. Her mouth was begging him to kiss her.

"Quiet on the set!" the producer shouted. "Roll tape in five, four…"

Katherine suddenly leaned forward, put her hand on Gray's knee, looked him in the eye and said, "It's just you and me. There's nothing to worry about."

"…two, one."

"Good evening. I'm Katherine Parsons. Tonight, we will be speaking to Gray North, the breakout star of Paul Stevens' movie *The Thunder Roared*. Welcome Gray."

"Thank you, Katherine. It's a pleasure to be here."

"Let's start with the easy questions, shall we? Is Gray North your real name?"

"Yes, it is. Gray, short for Graham."

"Born and raised in…"

"Detroit, Michigan."

"When you were 13 your parents separated. How did that effect you as a young man?"

"I didn't take it well. I began to act out, you know, petty crime, skipping school, poor grades. Pretty standard stuff I guess."

"What happened when you were 17?"

"I had been arrested again, that time for car theft. The Judge offered me a cell or a program. I opted for the program."

"What type of program?"

"It was a lock down. Involved intensive one-on-one and group counselling and acting exercises."

"How did you like that?"

"I wouldn't say that I liked it but, in retrospect, it was what I needed. I realized that if I stayed on my current path things would only get worse, I'd end up in jail or dead. I was headed for a dead-end."

"So, you left your old life behind and began to pursue acting, and, lucky for us." Katherine met his eyes and smiled.

"More like lucky for me."

"You do charity work with at risk youth. Tell me about that."

Gray began to relax. There was something about Katherine that seemed familiar. It put him at ease. She led him through his charity work; hit on his health and work out regimen; touched on his early acting gigs; and finished with *The Thunder Roared*.

"So, there you have it, Gray North, a bad boy made good. Good luck to you, Gray." Katherine smiled into the camera.

"Cut," the producer called.

Carly stood and unclipped her mic. First impressions, after all this time: Carly was breathless from Tap's magnetism. His sexy was rolling off of him and in her direction. He was wearing the outfit she had suggested, his hair was raked back, his green eyes were clear and alert.

"It was nice meeting you, Gray," she said.

"You too Katherine. I have to tell you I was pretty nervous about this interview," he said.

"I don't know why. You seem to be a pretty nice, genuine person."

"Well, thanks anyway."

"You're welcome," she responded.

Carly walked out of the studio. She walked straight to her office, closed the door and leaned against it. She had finally met her best friend. She did a little happy dance, opened the door and walked to production to review and edit the tape.

Mark, her producer, met her in the hallway. "That was quite the interview, Katherine," he said.

"Thanks, Mark," she responded.

"That wasn't a compliment."

"What do you mean?"

"I don't think you've ever done an interview like that, not that I can recall. Are you a fan or a journalist? Where were all the hard topics?"

"There were no hard topics. Gray is exactly what he appears to be: a nice guy."

"Really? No disgruntled girlfriends? No skeletons in his closet?"

"God, you are so jaded. Nice people do exist, Mark. You happened to have seen one today."

"I hope you're right, Katherine. If something pops up that you knew about but didn't pursue in this interview, well, it won't look good for you... or the show."

CHAPTER SEVEN

Friday night and Carly was headed out for drinks with an associate, Brad. They had started flirting a few weeks ago and he had finally asked her out. The plan was just drinks at Cobb's. She was looking forward to the evening, but not super excited. She had been single for months now and, although she was not desperate, maybe something could develop with Brad.

She arrived a fashionable ten minutes late and walked into Cobb's. The place was busy. Brad waved from a booth. She wove her way through the crowd. Brad stood up as she approached. She noticed that he looked her over from head to toe and when he smiled at her it was with admiration in his eyes. She smiled back and sat in the booth across from him.

"Wow, you look great, Katherine," he said.

"Thanks, Brad."

The waitress came to take her order.

"Two tequila shots," Brad interjected immediately.

"I'll have a light beer, doesn't matter which brand, surprise me," Carly said to the waitress. She turned to Brad, "shots? I wasn't planning that kind of an evening."

"A couple of shots will just loosen us up," he smiled at her, "make the conversation flow."

"Maybe you're right."

"Of course I'm right," he stated.

For some reason that annoyed Carly but she just put it down to nerves. Maybe Brad was nervous. It was their first date after all. He seemed different at work. If things got worse, she could just leave. Their drinks came, they did their shots and Brad ordered two more.

"So, what about you, Brad? What do you like to do in your free time?"

"I'm a sports fanatic! I watch it and play it. Football, baseball, golf, you name it, I do it. I played a lot of sports in high school, even got a baseball scholarship to university. Had hopes about going pro but I tore my rotator cuff in my final year."

"Wow, tough break."

"Yeah, well there's lots of guys out there with the same sad story, different version, but same ending."

Their shots arrived. Brad downed his immediately.

"C'mon, Katherine, down it," he encouraged her.

"I'm just going to let it sit for a bit Brad. Maybe later."

Suddenly there was a commotion at the door. Women were shouting and laughing, the volume in the bar amped up. Carly leaned out of the booth to look in that direction. Gray North had just walked in with some people, making their way to the bar to order drinks.

A trio of women walked up to him. He was smiling as he spoke to them. They gathered around him as he took a phone from one of them and put his arm out in front of himself to take a pic. The women crowded around him, he smiled at the phone, then one of the ladies reached in and grabbed his crotch. He gently removed her hand and said something to her. She laughed up at him, batting her eyes, and said something. He laughed, shook his head, took the pic and returned the phone to its owner. He began to turn back to face the bar and speak to his friends when his eyes met Carly's. He hesitated, smiled at her, and waved before completing his turn.

"You know him," Brad asked.

"No, I don't know him. I interviewed him on Wednesday," she responded as she reached for the shot glass and downed it in one gulp.

"You know he's looking over here," Brad said.

"So."

"Just saying, he's kinda giving me the look."

"What look?"

"You know, that guy look, like I'm talking to his girlfriend or whatever. You sure you don't know him?"

"It's just your imagination I'm sure. I don't know him. He wouldn't be looking at you like that," she reassured him.

Brad refocused on Carly. "So, what about you. What do you do in your spare time?"

Carly laughed. "Spare time? What's that? My job takes most of my spare time. I do a lot of research. When I do have a minute to myself I keep in touch with some friends from home."

"That's it? You don't knit or sew or hike or cook?"

Carly shook her head.

Brad caught the waitress' eye and held up two fingers. "Go to the movies?" he continued. "Shop? Run marathons?"

Carly continued to shake her head. The waitress came back to their table with two more shots. Brad picked up the glasses and handed one to Carly. She took it and he clinked his against hers.

"Bottoms up," he said and drained his glass.

Carly put her glass down on the table. She was already feeling the effects of the first two shots. This one might just put her over the top and she didn't want to go there with Brad. She was beginning to get an uncomfortable vibe from him. She would give him another half hour to see if things got any better.

"Not drinking," he said. "I didn't know you were a prude."

"I'm not a prude. I just don't want to get drunk. I don't generally drink this much this fast with someone I don't really know."

"You know me. We work together. You see me every day." He sounded annoyed.

"Katherine," someone said.

Carly turned her head to see a pair of washed-out jeans hugging muscular thighs. Her eyes climbed up a tight black t-shirt, stretched across a broad chest and shoulders, past a square jaw, a mischievous smile, into Gray North's green eyes.

"Mr. North, I saw you when you came in, hello."

Gray had sized up the guy Katherine was with, and he didn't like what he saw. He had also noticed her shaking her head to just about everything this guy had been saying to her. "You can call me Gray. Nice to see you. Everything okay over here?" That was an odd question, he knew.

"Of course, everything's okay," Brad snapped.

Gray ignored him, continuing to watch Katherine's face.

"Yes," she said, reaching for the shot glass. "Everything is fine. Thanks for asking." She took the shot and put the empty glass back on the table. Gray got a nervous vibe from Katherine. Was she nervous because he was speaking to her or was this guy making her nervous? He couldn't tell.

"Well okay then. I'm just here with a couple of buddies, having a few drinks," Gray said. There *was* something familiar about her. For some reason it made him feel protective of her. Too bad she was with this bonehead, but he had no say in her life.

"Yeah, we'll call you if we need you," Brad said snarkily.

Gray kept his eyes on Katherine. She seemed to be fine. He would keep tabs on her for the next little while anyway.

"Enjoy your evening, Gray," she said.

Gray left the table.

Carly quickly turned back to Brad. Not a good idea. That last shot hit her hard. She was a bit dizzy. "I'm going to visit the ladies' room." She slid out of the booth and took an unsteady step toward the bathroom.

Brad grabbed her wrist. "Don't forget to come back. I'll get us two more shots."

Carly pulled her wrist free and walked away. She went to the ladies' room. She leaned forward with her hands on the counter and took in several deep breaths. "I am not drunk, I am not drunk, I am not drunk," she repeated to herself. She needed to sober up. She needed to dump this guy and get the heck out of here.

Two more deep breaths and she opened the door. Gray North was standing in the hallway, waiting for her.

"That is definitely not the kind of guy I would picture you with Katherine," he said.

"I beg your pardon?" she asked.

"I would have thought someone with a bit more class maybe, someone a bit more like you."

"Maybe you don't know me as well as you seem to think you do. Maybe Brad is exactly the kind of guy I want," she responded.

"Is that so?"

"Yeah, what woman wouldn't want an alcoholic jerk?" she asked. And then she was laughing. She was laughing so hard, she fell into Gray's chest. "M-m-my dream man!" Another paroxysm of laughter. Brad was such a loser, and she was on a date with him. It was so sad it was hilarious. She put her hands on his hips to stop herself from sliding to the floor. Gray was chuckling along with her.

"You going to invite me to the wedding?" he asked.

"Sure! Why not? It'll be a destination wedding. The reception will be at a distillery in the Valley," she howled.

"Is Jack Daniels going to be the best man?"

"No, Jose Cuervo. My maid of honour will be Mai Tai."

"The flower girl will be Shirley Temple, of course." He had her in his arms, holding her up and laughing along with her now.

"Of course," she scoffed. "The bridesmaids will be dressed in champagne gowns."

"Will your Tia Maria be there as well?"

"Hell yes. My bouquet will be simple, four roses." Carly was gasping for breath. Her face hurt from laughing.

"What the fuck is this?" They both turned to see Brad standing in the hall glaring at them.

Carly looked at Brad, then looked at Gray, then back at Brad, and started laughing all over again. She was literally clinging to Gray. If she let go of him she would surely slide down his legs and land in a heap on the floor. Gray tightened his hold on her.

"What's your name? Is it Jim?" Gray asked. "Jim Beam?"

Carly let go of Gray and bent over laughing. Gray put his hand on her back.

"No. It's Brad Cummings, and that's my date your have your hands on."

"Date's over, buddy, time for Katherine to go home."

"That's funny, I didn't hear her say that."

"She just got a text from her uncle Tom Collins. He's screaming Bloody Mary because she's not home."

Two more zingers. Carly was going to pass out because she was laughing so hard. She took one hand off her knee and put it on Gray's chest. Leaning into him she pushed off his chest and stood up, a move she regretted when she staggered backward, pressing her entire body into his.

"St-st-stop. I can't breathe," she gasped. Gray put one of his arms around her waist. She tried to focus on Brad, but there seemed to be more than one of him. She didn't know which one to look at so she finally gave up and, instead, looked at Brad's shirt. "This isn't going to work for me, Brad. I'm so sorry… hic…really."

Brad was fuming. "Fucking bitch," he said as left.

"Oh, oh," Carly said. She turned toward Gray and whispered, "Brad's mad."

Gray whispered back, "He can go screwdriver himself. The night is still young, he may get lucky and have Sex on the Beach."

"You are killing me."

"Well, I don't want to do that. I think I should get you a cab. C'mon." Gray walked her back to her booth. "Did you drive here?"

"As a matter of fact, I did."

"Give me your keys then." He held out his hand.

"But my car…"

"Will be perfectly safe. I just don't want you to get any ideas. Keys."

Carly dug through her purse, located her keys, and placed them in his hand. He smiled down at her. "I'm going to call a cab but I need to speak to the people I came with. Don't go anywhere."

"You're as nice as I thought you would be," she slurred.

"Uhhh, okay."

Gray went to people he had arrived with and spoke to them while he motioned for the bartender. A few minutes later he was back at the booth.

"Let's go wait for your cab."

"Okay."

"You ready?"

"Locked and loaded."

Gray stopped. He looked down at Katherine. She was looking at him with puppy dog eyes. She couldn't be...could she? Gurl and Katherine Parsons were the same person? No. Why hadn't she said something earlier? It didn't make sense to him. Okay, this was one of those one in a million situations that some woman would respond to him like this. That had to be it. He would test her.

"Let's go," he said, holding out his hand, waiting for her response.

Katherine took his hand and, with his help, came out of the booth. She staggered into him and said, "Balls to the wall, Tap."

No way! "Gurl?"

"Yup!"

"What the... why didn't you..."

"I'm going to puke."

"You need some fresh air." He put his arm around her and walked her outside.

They had done a few laps from one end of the building to the other when the cab arrived. Gray had planned on putting her in the cab and returning to his friends. She seemed to be getting worse as the seconds ticked by on the way to the cab, so he climbed in the back with her. She gave the driver her address and fell over, her head in his lap.

Gray stroked her hair and rested his hand on her shoulder for the ride to her condo, all the while trying to wrap his head around the fact that Katherine Parsons was his Guerillagurl. He had questions for her but, she was in no condition to answer them.

When they arrived, he woke her up, told the driver to wait, and walked her into the foyer of her condo.

"Hey Tony!" Katherine called to the night doorman. She swayed toward Tony, but Gray held her upright.

"Ms Parsons, you okay?"

"I'm fine. I'm okay. I can't find my keys!" She gasped and looked up at Gray. "You have my keys," she slurred. "I can't get in without my keys."

"I'll take you up, don't worry about anything."

They got into the elevator. Katherine leaned against the back wall. When he opened her condo door, she ran past him to the bathroom and knelt in front of the toilet.

"You going to be okay?" he asked.

"Just go!" she yelled at him. "Don't look at me!"

"I'll just wait here for a couple of minutes to make sure you're okay," he said.

"No, please just g…"

Gray heard her throw up, and then mumble something. He walked to the bathroom and found her curled up on the floor. "You can't sleep in here Gurl," he said as he held out his hand to her. She reached up to grab his hand but missed. He took her hand and gently pulled her upright. "Where is your room, Gurl?"

Katherine mumbled again and pointed down the hall. He thought he had the right bedroom as it seemed to be more lived in.

He set her down on the end of her bed. She immediately flopped backward on the mattress. He smiled.

She looked adorable. He bent down, took off her shoes, and covered her with a quilt before quietly leaving and closing the condo door behind him.

CHAPTER EIGHT

Gray finished his workout, showered, and shaved. He left the hotel, got in Gurl's car and went through a drive-thru on the way to her condo. He parked in the visitor's parking stall and entered the foyer carrying a flat with two coffees.

"May I help you, sir?" the daytime doorman asked.

"I'm delivering Ms Parsons' car and coffee. I know the way."

"I'm sorry but I'm going to have to call Ms Parsons before I let you in," he said.

"Yeah, she's probably still sleeping. Late night. I'll just go up."

"I can't let you do that."

"Listen, I'm already late and she is going to be pissed when she finds out that you wouldn't let me in. Trust me, bro, you don't want to have to deal with that," Gray said. He smiled at the doorman. "I don't usually say this but, you do know who I am don't you?"

"I recognize you Mr. North."

"Ms Parsons and I are old friends. There won't be a problem, unless you make one. You can even come up with me if you'd like."

Just then a lady walked into the foyer. "Doug, get my bags would you?" she called to the doorman.

"Yes, Mrs. Williams." He scurried out from behind the desk.

Mrs. Williams spared a glance at Gray. She did a double take. "Are you?"

"Yes, ma'am, I am. Pleased to meet you."

"I'm a huge fan, do you mind?" she asked as she pulled a cell out of her purse.

"Not at all." Still carrying the flat of coffee, he put his arm around Mrs. Williams' shoulders and bent down while she snapped a pic. "I've got to go. I'm late for an appointment," he said. He went to the elevator, got in, and pushed the button for Gurl's floor.

The elevator opened on 15. Tap went to Gurl's door and rang the buzzer. He waited a minute and pressed it again. He waited another minute and leaned on it.

"Just a minute," Gurl called.

He could hear her on the other side of the door mumbling something.

"What?" The door swung open. Gurl stood there in an oversized t-shirt, boxer shorts and sunglasses. Her hair was sticking up in all directions. She looked like she had just rolled out of bed, which, he assumed, she had. "Oh God," she said when she saw him.

"No, just Gray," he smiled. He held out the flat of coffee. "Did you order a double double?"

Carly stepped out of the way, holding the door open for Tap. He walked in. She grabbed a coffee from the tray as he passed her. "Thank you," she said. "C'mon," she walked down the hall, through the living room/kitchen, to a wall of windows. She slid open a door and walked out onto a large balcony where she plopped onto a lounger. She motioned to the lounger beside her and leaned back.

Tap stood over her, looking down. He put his finger on the bridge of her sunglasses and slid them down to the tip of her nose. She looked up at him with bloodshot eyes. "Ouch," he said as he sat on the lounger beside her.

"Yeah. No need to yell by the way," she said as she pushed the glasses back up her nose. "What are you doing here anyway?"

"It's Saturday," he replied in a tone that implied she should know something.

"And..." she prompted.

"We always chat on Saturday mornings. I thought I would come by so we could do it in person."

"Oh." Using both hands she brought the coffee cup to her lips and took a tentative sip. "Ummm. This is just what I needed." She smiled. So far so good. She had been afraid that finally meeting Tap would be a disappointment, that maybe she wouldn't like him after all. But no, she liked him as much in person as over the phone. Having him here on Saturday morning was the most natural thing in the world. If she wasn't so hung over, she probably would have hugged him at the door but just putting one foot in front of the other and finally making it to her destination was effort enough.

"Why didn't you tell me who you were at the interview?" Tap asked.

"I don't know. It didn't seem like the right time or place."

"When was the right time and where was the right place going to be?"

"Something else in a long list of questions I don't know the answer to." She put her cup down and sagged into the lounger even more. "I really like it here in the mornings."

Tap nodded his head. "Yeah, nice view."

"And quiet. You'd never know there was a city of more than four million people down there. Probably two million dogs too."

"Different from New York, that's for sure. More people, more noise, not as many dogs but more rats."

"Yikes. Really?"

"I don't know. They won't sit still. Makes it hard to count them."

"Goof."

"How are Melissa and Brittany?"

"Great. Melissa is still seeing Barry. Brittany got that job she was hoping to get. Did you get your workout in yet?"

"Yeah, this morning before I came. There's a pretty good gym at the hotel."

"That's nice."

"Do you have anything to eat? I should have picked up something on the way here."

"I have stuff for me to eat. I don't know if my stuff is up to your high nutritional standards though. Go take a look."

Tap stood and went into the kitchen. Carly felt like she was sinking deeper into the lounger. She closed her eyes for a brief moment listening to him opening the cupboards in the kitchen.

"Hey, do you want an egg white omelette?"

Carly didn't answer.

Tap walked out onto the balcony to find Gurl asleep. He looked at her with affection. Wow, this was Gurl. He was here in person, with his best friend. How perfect was that? There had been no awkwardness between them.

Tap went back into the kitchen to make an omelette for himself. Afterward he cleaned up and toured the apartment. He picked up and looked at the pictures she had displayed. He guessed these were her parents. These two had to be Melissa and Brittany. Who was who though? He didn't know. He couldn't remember which was the blonde and which was the redhead.

He came to a large abstract painting on the wall. This was the first real piece of art she had purchased. He remembered her telling him about it. She really liked it, liked the colours and shapes. When she had hung it on the wall, that was the first time she had felt like a grown up. She was in her own condo, hanging a piece of art that she loved, in the place that she wanted it to go. He smiled.

He took a quick peek into the bathroom. Guest bath, tastefully decorated. He was not surprised. Down the hall to two bedrooms, one with a queen bed, the other with two twins. Guest rooms.

Lastly, he stood in the doorway to her bedroom. The bed was unmade since he had woken her up when he arrived. It would be creepy for him to go in, so he stayed where he was. But he chuckled when he saw Bingo on the floor, her blue teddy bear that she had brought from home and who kept her company when she was feeling home sick.

A couple of hours later Gurl's breathing changed. Tap knew she was waking up. She stretched her arms, then her legs and torso. Finally, she turned her head in his direction. Suddenly she sat up.

"You're really here? I thought I was dreaming."

"You and every other hot-blooded woman in the world, baby."

"In the world? You have to work on that low self-esteem of yours, Tap."

"I'm tryin'." He gave her a dazzling smile. "You hungry? You slept through an incredible omelette by the way."

"Don't mention eggs. I'm not ready for that yet. I'm going to make some toast though." She stood up and saw her reflection in the patio windows. "Good God, my hair!"

Tap smiled at her affectionately. "Listen, I'll make the toast. Why don't you go shower, Katherine? You'll feel better."

"Yeah, I will. Thanks, Tap. By the way my friends call me Carly. You can call me Ms Parsons." She giggled. "For real, you can call me Carly."

Carly took a shower, got dressed and fixed her hair. She came out of her bedroom in baggy brown shorts, a black silk shell and a straw fedora. Toast and coffee were waiting for her on the granite island.

"Hey," she said to Tap. "I'm meeting some friends for lunch. They would love to meet you. Why don't you tag along?"

"What kind of people? I'm not really dressed for a public appearance."

"Just friends. Your kind of people, by the way—performers and writers. I'll take you to your hotel so you can get changed and then we can go."

Julie sat in her car. She had paid the doorman good money for the information she got. She had been sitting there for hours. She would be sitting there for hours more, although she hoped she wouldn't have to.

The door to the building opened. Katherine Parsons and Gray North strolled out. Julie picked up her camera and started shooting. Katherine Parsons and Gray North. Who woulda thunk it?

Julie turned the key in her ignition and slowly pulled out of her parking stall to trail them.

CHAPTER NINE

On the way to Gray's hotel, Carly drove him past some landmarks and a few of her favourite places. When they arrived at his hotel, she told him she would wait in the lobby and that he should take his time.

"Don't be ridiculous. Come up," he insisted.

The elevator doors opened on his floor. He preceded her down the hall. He held the door open for her and she entered a lavish sitting room. Carly sat down while Tap gathered some things and went to take a shower. The bathroom door closed. Carly stood. Tap's jacket was thrown over the back of the couch. She picked it up and smelled it. Smelled good.

She stood in the doorway to the bedroom. His suitcase was opened. He hadn't bothered to unpack his clothes. She walked in. He had left a pair of loafers at the foot of his bed. She slipped off her shoe and put her foot in his loafer. It was big. Putting her shoe back on she walked over to his suitcase and gently ran her hand over the neatly packed clothes. There was a bottle of cologne on the dresser. She picked it up and smelled it.

"You like it?" Tap asked. He walked into the bedroom. His hair was damp and combed back from his face. His chiseled torso was bare, a towel was wrapped dangerously low around his hips.

"Yeah," Carly replied. "I don't recognize this fragrance." She put the bottle down.

"That's no fragrance, Gurl, that's cologne. Man smell."

She rolled her eyes. "Whatever… What are you doing?" she shrieked.

Tap was unwrapping the towel. He looked up at her. "Getting dressed."

"Wha… not in front of me!" She hurried out of the room.

"Sorry," he said, chuckling. He leaned over and pushed the door closed.

Forty-five minutes later they entered Coco's and walked toward the back. People were squeezed in around three tiny tables that had been pushed together. There was more than one lively conversation going on.

Carly stood at one end, coughed, and said, "Hey, everyone, I'd like you to meet my best friend, Gray North."

All discussion ceased. Shocked faces stared at her, eyes darted from her to Gray and then from Gray to her.

"Oh come on! Like you haven't seen a movie star before." Carly said. "Squinch over people, we need two more chairs here." She grabbed a chair for herself and pointed to another for Gray. He pulled it over. Everybody moved to make room. It was a tight fit, but they made it work.

The waitress came over. "The usual for me, Theresa," Carly said. "What do you want, Tap?"

"I'll have an Americano, two milks please, Theresa." He smiled at her. Theresa turned red.

Carly introduced them. "Theresa, Gray; Gray, Theresa,

best waitress in L.A." Then she started on the table, "Gray, this is Sherri Gomez, screenwriter; Colin Gordon, actor; Jessie Bodner, actress and Colin's wife; John Cho, comedian; Terry Thompson, writer; Greg Chappel, writer and Terry's partner; Margo Simms, actress; Stacey Edwards, poet; Josh Anderson, musician, drummer, and I think that's it."

"No introduction needed for me," a voice said from behind them. Paul Stevens, the director of Tap's movie, put his hand on Gray's shoulder. "I didn't know you knew Carly."

"Uh, I didn't know either—strange, I know," Gray looked at Carly. She shrugged her shoulders then moved her chair over, starting the whole chain to rearrange and make room for Paul.

Their coffees came and Paul placed his order. The conversation stalled as their orders were delivered, but it didn't take long before everyone was talking. Paul was speaking to Sherri about the script she was working on. Margo and Jessie were talking about an audition they were going to go to on Tuesday. John was speaking to Terry about writing some jokes for him. Carly was telling Greg about her disastrous date on Friday. Josh was talking to Stacey about using her poems as songs. Colin was speaking to Gray about his big break into show business and whether New York was an easy market to break into.

Gray was enjoying himself. He had worried that maybe this whole event would focus on him as a celebrity, and he hadn't wanted that. He put his arm around Gurl as he leaned over her to ask Sherri about her script. Later, when he asked Theresa for a bottle of water, he put his hand on Gurl's knee, squeezed it, and left it there. He wanted to touch her and couldn't seem to keep his hands to himself. She accepted his hand on her knee. They all laughed at something that Josh said when she laid her hand on top of his before reaching forward for her coffee.

It was early evening when everyone started leaving. Carly and Gray walked out of the café and stood on the street. She leaned her head back and took a deep breath. Gray stuffed his hands in his pockets to keep them off her.

"I guess I'll take you back to your hotel," she said.

"Sure."

"I don't really want the day to end though," she confessed to him.

"Do you have anything in mind? I don't have anywhere to be. We can still hang."

"I do have an idea. C'mon."

They got in the car and Carly drove farther out into the suburbs, not noticing the car following them. She pulled into a strip mall, and they got out of the car.

"This way," she said as she put her hand out to Gray.

Gray took her hand then pulled her to his side and put his arm around her neck. "Lead the way."

She put her arm around his waist. "Are you this handsy with all your friends?" she asked.

"I could ask you the same question," he said. "But, no, my guy friends hate it when I do this kind of stuff."

Carly laughed. It was just so natural for them to be together. She didn't feel crowded or uncomfortable when Gray touched her or pulled her close. It was like she belonged there with him.

Gray felt the same way. She fit him perfectly in every way. He couldn't help himself. It was almost like he didn't believe that she was really his Gurl and that they were finally together in person. He had to keep touching her to convince himself that she was real.

Carly steered Gray toward the middle of the strip mall toward a brightly lit façade. Gray read the name of the store. "No way," he said.

"Way," Carly said. "You're not scared, are you?"

"Scared of what?" he scoffed.

"That I'll kick your ass, that's what."

"As if, Gurl. You're the one who's going to be crying on the way home," he said as he pushed the door to the arcade open.

They spent hours playing games, shooting aliens, driving race cars and motorcycles, shooting hoops. Carly was winning. Then Gray would take the lead. They seesawed and eventually decided to call it a tie. They pooled their tickets and got neon plastic bracelets, his was green, hers was yellow.

CHAPTER TEN

The next morning Carly picked up Gray and drove him to the beach. They jogged at the ocean's edge for miles, passing other joggers, walkers, dogs and fishermen. When they returned to the car, they opened the trunk and pulled out a couple of beach chairs, a blanket, towels, a cooler and a bag. Returning to the beach they picked their spot. Gray dug into the bag and pulled out a thermos and some cups. He poured some coffee, and they sat in silence, watching the people and drinking their coffee.

The sun was bright, and the temperature was rising. Carly stood, unzipped her jacket and took off her jogging pants. She wore a white bikini with frills at the neckline of the top and the waistline of the bottoms. Gray gasped when he saw what she was wearing. He thought she looked heavenly. He also thought the bikini would look better on the floor of his bedroom. What? Where did that come from?

Carly pulled a bottle of sunblock out of the bag, squirted a healthy blob onto her hand and began applying it to her legs and arms.

"Get my back, will you?" she asked, kneeling in front of Gray. She handed him the sunblock and turned with her back to him. Gray applied the sunblock in long smooth strokes. Carly moaned and leaned back into his hands. "That's nice."

Gray's hands were warm on her back. He reached up and smoothed the lotion on her shoulders and down her back again. If she were to turn just six inches to the right, he would be massaging her breast.

Carly suddenly felt hot. *What are you thinking?* she chastised herself.

"I'll do you now," Carly said quickly.

Gray stood and pulled his t-shirt off. She stood behind him, running both hands down his back, admiring his physique and his tight ass. She shook her head to clear it. "All done."

They lay side-by-side on the blanket, warmed by the sun, people watching.

"So," Gray said at last, "you know Paul Stevens."

"Yes I do."

"Known him for long?"

"Since I moved here, so a couple of years."

"You knew about the script, didn't you? That's why you sent me to meet him."

"Yes. Does that bother you?"

"No. It just didn't occur to me that you knew him that well, that's all. Thanks, by the way."

"No problem. I was happy to help you both." Carly flipped over so she was lying on her back. "Hey, about Friday night..."

"No, I don't think you should go out with Brad again."

"That's not what I was going to say."

Gray rolled to his side, leaning on his elbow as he looked at her. "What were you going to say?"

"I was...."

"Cuz, just ask."

"I know, when..."

"I'm an open book, Gurl. I'll tell you whatever you want to know."

"Okay, thanks, but when we..."

"Don't be shy, blurt it out."

"Friday night..."

"I'm here for you Gurl. Just ask."

Carly was laughing. "I would ask if you would let me finish."

"Okay. Serious now. Ask."

"That lady at the bar, the one that grabbed your package. Does that happen to you all the time?"

"Not all the time. More times than I care for though."

"Do you like that?"

"Would you like it if some strange guy came up to you and grabbed your boob?"

"No, that's gross. But you can't deny you like the ladies, Tap. It must save you a lot of time and effort if women just offer themselves to you like that."

"Yeah, it does save time and effort, but they generally don't want me. They want to do Chief Officer Scott. They usually want to act out their favourite scene and expect me to remember the dialogue. It's actually kind of creepy."

"But you have taken some of those offers?"

"Would a sugar addict say 'no' to free day at a candy store? Of course I have."

"Oh, you ho," she teased.

"Don't judge, Gurl," he responded with a smirk.

Gray stood and held out his hand to Carly. "C'mon. It's getting hot. Let's go in the water."

Carly took his hand. Gray pulled her up, bent down, and threw her over his shoulder. He started running for the water.

"No," she shrieked, "put me down."

"I'll put you down all right. You're goin down, Gurl!" he yelled back at her.

Carly pounded on his back, "Don't dunk me! Put me down."

Gray ran into the surf, splashing them both. He waded deeper until the water was up to his waist. Carly screamed the whole way. He fell backward, releasing Carly and dropping her into the water. He came up laughing. She came up sputtering.

"You're going to die for that!" she screamed, running at him. He took off, Carly in hot pursuit. She caught up and launched herself at his back, pushing him under.

"That's the way it's going to be?" he asked when he came up.

She was backing away from him slowly. "You know you deserved it!" she yelled. She turned and drove into the water, swimming frantically.

He dove in right behind her. She would pay!

They played in the water for hours, splashing, yelling and laughing.

• • •

Julie sat on the beach under an umbrella and a big floppy hat, her camera incessantly clicking. This was as good as money in the bank. If she could get a picture of them kissing, she would probably get the lead on the next show. But no such luck. Still, Gray was hot right now. This story would bring in viewers just to hear about him and see pictures of him in his trunks.

Chapter Eleven

The next day was Monday. Back to reality for Carly. The weekend had been great. Tap was great. They had had so much fun together. She spent the day working on her next interview. She searched the internet, did telephone interviews, read news articles, and wrote her first draft of questions.

She got home, slipped off her shoes and dumped her purse and papers on the dining room table. Straight to the bathroom for a shower and then to the kitchen to do something for supper. The intercom buzzed.

"Hello."

"Ms Parker, Gray North is here to see you. Should I send him up?"

"Definitely."

She picked up the remote and turned on the tv on the way to the foyer. She unlocked the door and headed back to the kitchen. She looked in the freezer to see what she could quickly heat up.

"Hello," Gray called from the foyer.

"Kitchen," she called back.

Gray walked in the kitchen and smiled at her. She was about to say something to him when something on the tv caught her attention:

"Gray North is in town. Who is he spending his time with? Is this the new lady in Gray's life?"

Gray and Carly looked at each other, then turned toward the tv. There was a picture of them walking into the arcade, his arm looped around her neck, her arm around his waist.

"What the…" Gray said.

"Oh my God," Carly said.

They both sat on the couch watching the celebrity news show. The reporters were gathered in their studio, talking about the video clips and photos they had taken that day. The show was going to break for commercials but, before the break, another teaser ran for Gray's story. They didn't speak, they didn't move, they were glued to the tv.

Commercials over, the show came back on. The host spoke.

"Janice, what do you have for us?" he asked.

"Well, Gray North is in town doing interviews for *The Thunder Roared*. He was interviewed by Katherine Parsons last week and… guess who Gray has been spending all his spare time with?"

Another picture of her and Gray flashed on the screen. They were coming out of her condo building. The next picture was of them walking into his hotel. The picture after that was them walking out. Gray had different clothes on.

"They spent the weekend together," Janice said. "They are a cute couple. They met friends at Coco's, went to an arcade. They were at the beach on Sunday."

Several pictures of them at the beach came on screen.

"It was like watching two puppies play in the water," Janice said.

"I can't believe he would date Katherine Parsons," one of the other reporters said. "He better hope that when they break up it's on good terms."

Another reporter added, "Yeah, one place you do not want to be is on Katherine Parsons' bad side. Gray, buddy, watch your back."

"C'mon guys," the host said. "She can't be that bad. He looks pretty happy. Maybe she has a soft side. She can't be business all the time."

"I'd let her all up in my business," another of the guys said. "Look at how she fills out that bikini."

"Yeah, she's rocking that thing," Janice said. "They are like the perfect couple. Gray's looking pretty hot himself, all shirtless and shtuff."

"Calm down, Janice," the host joked. "Tom, who did you run into at the airport?"

Tom took the lead, showing his video. Gray and Carly remained motionless on the couch, neither of them speaking. Carly's phone rang, breaking their paralysis. She picked it up. Gray listened to her side of the conversation.

"Hello?"

"Hi Dad."

"You saw that?"

"Actually, I do know him. Gray is Tap."

"Really!"

"Yes… yes… no… yes, he's here right now. I don't know," she turned to Gray. "Why are you here?"

"I thought we could hang out."

"We're going to hang out... I don't know," she turned to Gray again. "What do you mean hang out?"

Gray took the phone from Carly. "Hello, Sir... yes, it's a pleasure to finally speak to you as well... yes... I just got here actually, we haven't discussed anything yet..." He looked over at Carly. "Well, I think she just got home from work... I don't think she has had dinner yet... yes...okay."

He returned the phone to Carly.

"Okay Dad... Say hi to Mom... Love you too... Bye." She ended the call.

"Have you eaten yet?" she asked Gray.

The phone rang again. It was Melissa.

"Melissa! You saw that? Yes... yes... He's here now... We're gonna hang out... No, I don't know."

Gray stood up and went to the kitchen.

Carly was talking to Melissa on the phone. She heard Gray rustling around in the cupboards. The fridge opened and closed a couple of time. Her phone beeped, indicating a call on the other line.

"Wait," she said to Melissa, "Brittany's on the other line. Let me conference." She pulled the phone away from her ear, pushed a couple of buttons. "Brittany... Don't you people have anything better to do than watch gossip tv?" Carly laughed. "Melissa's on this call too."

A pan hit the stove. Something started sizzling.

"O.M.G! Why would you ask that? You guys are awful," Carly laughed. "Hey, Gray, say hi to Melissa and Brittany," she called.

"Hello, Melissa and Brittany," Gray called back. He could hear screaming coming from the phone. He smiled.

"Stop it," Carly said. "Yes, I'll let you guys know about tonight. But enough about me and my fifteen minutes of fame. What's happening with you two?"

Half an hour later, Gray interrupted Carly. "Supper's ready."

"Yes, he said supper's ready... I don't know what he made... I don't know...Okay. Love you guys. We'll talk soon." Carly ended the call.

She turned toward the kitchen. There were two plates set out, two glasses of wine.

"Tap, you are a life saver! Thank you so much."

Carly hugged him. He returned the embrace and pulled out a bar stool for her. He sat next to her.

"Do we need to discuss this?" Carly asked.

"No, I think my cooking skills speak for themselves." He smiled at her.

"Not dinner, which is excellent by the way, the show."

"Ah yes. The show." He paused. "What's to discuss? They have the photos, we weren't doing anything wrong. No, there is nothing to discuss."

Gray and Carly were featured every night for the next week. Gray entering her condo; them leaving together; them at Stacey's slam reading; them at dinner with Paul; them shopping at a farmer's market; them bouncing up and down on the dance floor at one of Josh's gigs.

Saturday morning came, and they were on Carly's balcony again drinking coffee, courtesy of Gray.

"Got a call from my agent yesterday," Gray said.

"Yeah?"

"I've got to go back to New York for a bit. Someone has requested a meeting. She wouldn't say who or why but she hinted that I wouldn't want to miss it." Gray had been hesitant to tell Carly and he didn't know why he felt that way. He didn't want to go back to New York yet. He was having so much fun with her. He could move things around to take more time off and stay here.

Carly was surprised and disappointed that their time together was going to end so soon. "When are you going?"

"Tomorrow afternoon."

"How long are you going to be gone?"

"I don't know. I don't know what the meeting is about." Gray wanted to tell her that he would be back as soon as possible but he couldn't tell her that because he didn't know. He was going to miss her. He couldn't tell her that either.

Carly didn't respond. What could she say? Don't go? She had no right to ask him that. They were just friends, that's all. She was going to miss him, but she couldn't tell him that.

"Hey," Gray said, "why don't you come with? I can show you around the Big Apple. Return the favour."

"I can't, Tap. I have to work."

"You always have an excuse, Gurl. Don't you have any vacation time? C'mon," he reached over and shook her shoulder. "You know you want to."

"I do want to but I can't. Not right now. I'm finishing up an interview. We tape on Wednesday. Once that is done you'll have had your meeting and if you are going to be in New York for longer I'll see about taking a week."

"Promise?" he asked.

"Promise," she responded.

The next day Carly drove Gray to the airport. She got out of the car and opened the trunk. He pulled out his suitcase and set it on the pavement. He put his hands on her shoulders and pulled her into a hug. He rested his chin on the top of her head. What was he going to do without her?

Carly let go and stepped away. She looked up into his green eyes. Good God, was she going to start crying? She quickly looked down.

"Yeah, I can't park here. I gotta go."

"I know."

"Hey, it's not like we'll never see each other again. You've got my number, I've got yours. We'll text and talk."

"Of course!"

She gave him another quick hug, got into her car, leaned over, waved, and drove away. Gray took the handle to his suitcase and walked into the airport.

"Where you going, Gray?"

Janice was standing in front of him, a cameraman behind her.

"Janice, you are spending way too much time following me around," he said.

"Where are you going?"

"New York."

"Is Katherine Parsons joining you there?"

"I don't know. Is she?"

"You tell me. She's your girlfriend."

"She's not my girlfriend, Janice. She is my friend, my best friend."

"Are you coming back to L.A.?"

"Some day, yes. I enjoyed my stay."

"Because of Katherine?"

"I think they're calling my flight."

That clip played on Monday night. One of the other female reporters stated, "I want to be Gray North's best friend too."

"Doesn't everyone," Janice responded.

CHAPTER TWELVE

The next week was busy for Carly and Gray. Aside from the usual activities of having their respective lives, they were busy with business. Carly finalized her interview and taped on Wednesday. Gray's meeting had been postponed to the next week. He did an interview and photo shoot for a men's fitness magazine and met with his agent. The down time was the worst. Gray felt as if there was nothing to look forward to at the end of the day. Carly's life seemed a bit duller without Gray at her side. They continued to text and Skype, and those were the highlights of their days.

Early Friday morning, Carly was meeting with her assistant discussing what their next interview would be. Carly's cell rang. She picked it up and saw Gray's number. She put him on speaker.

"Hey, Tap!"

"Hey, yourself."

"Say hi to Rosie, we're talking about my next interview."

"Hi, Rosie."

Rosie blushed. "Hi, Gray," she responded.

Carly held up her hand. "Give me five, Rosie," she said. Rosie left her office, closing the door behind her.

"What's happening in New York?" Carly asked.

"Oh, you know, the usual, gym, meeting with my

agent, reading scripts, beating off women; what else? Umm, a meeting with Carlos Garcea and Ken Curtis."

Carlos Garcea was an established director and Ken Curtis one of the hottest actors, a guaranteed box office hit, popular with men and women. Carlos and Ken had collaborated on more than one film. Each one of them were huge money makers. Each one of them had boosted the careers of co-stars.

"No way," Carly said.

"Way," Gray responded. There was an edge of excitement in his voice.

"What did they want? Spill."

"They're doing another movie. They want me to co-star!" he shouted into the phone.

"Yes! Congratulations Tap. Good for you."

"I told them I would think about it."

"You… what? What did you say?"

"I told them I would think about it. You know, give them an answer in a couple of days."

"Are you insane?"

"No. I'm an actor, and I just acted as if I didn't say yes immediately. Of course I took the part."

"You goof. I'm so happy for you, Tap."

"Really?"

"Truly."

"How happy?"

"Very happy."

"Happy enough to come to New York to celebrate?"

Carly's heart soared at the invitation. "Yes. Yes. I'll come to New York." She missed being with Gray. She had just gone over her calendar with Rosie and knew that she had some time to spare.

A wave of relief washed over Gray. Gurl was coming to New York. "Let me know when you'll be here. I'll pick you up at the airport."

They ended the call. Carly called Rosie back into her office.

"Get me to New York as soon as possible. I want to leave today, the sooner the better," she told her.

"What about a hotel? Where do you want to stay?"

"Damn. I don't know exactly where Gray lives. I'll call and ask what's close to his place… I'll take care of that Rosie. Thanks."

Rosie left her office. Carly closed her laptop and went to her producer's office to tell him she was going to be unavailable for the next week as of right now. She went home to pack. Rosie called her and told her she had a flight booked for 4:45 p.m. She would be in New York by 10:00 p.m. Carly called a cab, did one last run through of her apartment to make sure she hadn't forgotten anything, then closed her suitcase and called Tap from the elevator.

Carly arrived in New York at 9:50. Tap was waiting for her. He pulled her into a big hug, kissing her forehead. Tension that he had been unaware of, flowed out of his body.

Carly returned his hug and looked up at him when he kissed her forehead. She smiled. She felt as if she was finally home. They looked at each other, smiling for maybe a minute longer than necessary. Gray finally released her. He took her hand and lead her to the incoming luggage carousel. They got her suitcase and caught a cab.

"Where you staying?" Tap asked.

"I'm... shit. I was in such a rush I forgot to call you about a hotel. What's a good hotel close to where you live? Let's see if I can get a room."

Tap gave the cabbie an address as they drove away from the airport.

"Is that close to your place?" Carly asked.

"Yeah. Couldn't be any closer," Tap said. "You're staying with me."

"No, I don't want to be a bother."

"You are a bother, but I'm going to put up with you for the next week because I want to. Don't make me regret it," he teased.

"Thanks, Tap, but..."

"But what? Discussion over. You're staying at my place."

Tap's apartment was a small two bedroom on the third floor of a brownstone. It was furnished with an assortment of furniture, nothing matched. A bookcase had been constructed with 1x6s nailed to the wall. It was stacked with books, movies, video games, Star Trek action figures and assorted other things.

"It's humble, but it's home," Gray said.

"I love it."

He took her down a short hallway, bedroom on the

right, bathroom on the left, guest room at the end. He flicked a switch on the wall and put her suitcase on the bed.

"This is nice," she said.

Gray pulled her into another hug. "This is nice," he said. "C'mon, let's go."

"Go where?"

"To celebrate. I've got some friends waiting for me. You're coming to meet the gang."

"I can't go anywhere looking like this!"

"You look great."

"Oh please! Give me five minutes." She stepped away from him, grabbed her purse and went into the bathroom.

He followed her down the hall. She put her purse on the toilet, pulled out her brush and ran it through her hair. She put the brush back and pulled out a small bag. She opened it and started to refresh her makeup. He smiled watching her. She reapplied lipstick, gloss, and then smacked her lips together.

That looks tasty, Gray thought to himself. If this wasn't Gurl, he would probably be nuzzling her neck right about now. He had to stop these thoughts. He didn't want to ruin his friendship with Gurl. What if she didn't share his attraction and think he was some sort of creep? He didn't want to chance it.

Carly repacked her makeup bag and put it back in her purse.

"Ready," Gray asked.

She looked at him and smiled. "Locked and loaded."

"Let's go." He held out his hand.

"Balls to the wall, Tap," she said as she took his hand and slung her purse over her shoulder.

CHAPTER THIRTEEN

The bar was busy, packed with people. They entered and someone shouted, "Gray!" There was a group of people standing and sitting around a table covered with beer bottles.

Holding her hand, Gray lead Carly through the crowd to the table. "I'm here," he said. He pulled Carly to his side, "and she's here, safe and sound."

Introductions were made: Roger, fellow actor; Brett, sound technician; Patti, makeup and Brett's girlfriend; Tom, an accountant; Jessie, Tom's wife; and Luke, fellow actor. These were fellow actors, technicians, friends and spouses/girlfriends. Introductions were done, drinks were ordered, the music was pounding. Gray grabbed her hand again and pulled her onto the dance floor.

They returned to the table for a breather and a drink. One of Tap's friends stood and offered Carly his seat. She sat. Tap stood behind her, his hand on her shoulder. She picked up her bottle and took a swig. She put her bottle down on the table. Luke leaned over and shouted into her ear, "Let's dance!"

Carly laughed, stood and went to dance with Luke. Tap turned to watch them go. Patti touched his arm. He bent down to hear her.

"She seems nice, Gray. How long have you known her?"

"I've known her since I was twelve or thirteen."

"What! Why is this the first time we've met her?"

"She lives in L.A. Meeting just never worked out before. I was working, she was in school, then we were both broke, then she was working and on and on."

"Too bad. You are a cute couple."

"We're not a couple, Patti. We're just friends. Best friends."

"Coulda fooled me."

"Hey," he looked at her and smiled, "I'm not ready to settle down yet."

The song ended. Luke and Carly returned to the table. Carly picked up her purse and walked to the bathroom. She needed a breather! *So far, so good*, she thought as she refreshed her makeup and brushed her hair. Gray's friends seemed nice, and she was having a good time.

She came out of the bathroom and stepped into the bar.

"Let's dance," someone said to her.

She turned to the voice. A very attractive man was looking at her.

"Uh, thanks, but I'm here with friends."

He stepped toward her. "You're not allowed to dance with anyone else?"

"No, it's not that, it's just that I want to spend time with my friends."

"One dance won't hurt anything," he pressed her.

"Yeah, I know, but, no."

"C'mon babe, you know you want to," he leered at her.

"You want to what, Carly?" Gray asked from behind her.

"I don't want to anything Gray," she said.

"I didn't think so," he said glaring at the other man. "C'mon," he put his arm around Carly's shoulders, and they returned to the table.

After the bar they all went to a diner for French fries and burgers. Gray sat beside Carly, his arm around the back of her chair. The conversation flowed along with the jokes and laughs. It was very early in the morning when they all went their separate ways.

Neither Carly nor Gray were up to greet the sun. It was early afternoon before Gray finally got up and made himself a cup of coffee. He took a sip, savoring the flavour. He heard the bathroom door close. He automatically made a second cup of coffee. Carly came into the kitchen. He handed her the mug and waited while she added milk and sugar. He took her hand, led her out of his apartment and up the stairs to a roof top terrace. They sat beside each other enjoying their coffee, not speaking, listening to the traffic, dogs barking and kids playing.

"How are you feeling this morning?" Gray broke the silence.

"Good. Happy." She turned her head and smiled at him.

"Let's hang here for a bit. Then we can go out for a while. Sound okay?"

"Sounds perfect."

They caught a double decker bus tour of New York, went for a late lunch at a famous deli and ended the day at the Museum of Natural History. They returned to Gray's apartment and got changed for dinner.

Carly walked into the living room in a red halter dress that draped loosely, ending several inches above the knee.

Gray gasped. She looked at him. He was in a suit, a spotless white dress shirt and patterned burgundy and white tie. She lifted her eyebrows.

"Not so bad yourself, Tap," she said.

He laughed. "Ready?"

"Locked and loaded."

"Let's go."

"Balls to the wall." They both laughed.

Carly proceeded Gray out of the apartment and down the stairs to the street. They caught a cab to a five-star restaurant. Dinner, dessert, wine and three hours later they left the restaurant.

Gray put his hand on the small of her back, guiding her down the street. "Let's walk. I need to work off some of that dinner."

He put his arm around her and, as they walked, he told her about some of the shops in the area. He pointed to a restaurant with a closed sign hanging on the door. That was where he got his first job in New York waiting tables. This bodega was where he used to buy mac and cheese and Ramen noodles to get him through the week. The people were really nice. Favourite coffee shop over there. His first hole-in-the-wall apartment was over that shop.

Carly knew of these places from her discussions with Tap. It was nice to finally see them.

They cabbed back to Gray's apartment. They ended the day with Carly lying on the couch, her head on Gray's lap, watching a movie.

CHAPTER FOURTEEN

When Carly woke up the next morning the apartment was empty. She walked into the kitchen and found a note from Gray: *At the gym.*

She thought of walking to a nearby diner for coffee, but she didn't have a key to his apartment. Instead, she made herself a coffee. She browsed the bookcase. She took out some books, read the backs and returned them to their spot. She recognized the video games and smiled. She went to Gray's bedroom and stood in the doorway. His bed was made, the dresser was organized. The room was tidy, no clothes on the floor or the single chair in the corner.

By the time she finished her coffee and got dressed Gray was back from the gym. He was a sweaty mess. He dropped his gym bag at the door and met her in the kitchen.

"Morning, Gurl." He squeezed by her, pulled a bottle of water out of the fridge, opened it and drank deeply.

Carly closed her eyes. His smell enveloped her. If she stuck out her tongue, she would probably be able to taste it. She knew it would taste good... *Stop that!* If this was not Gray, she might hug him and breathe him in. But this was Tap and that would be awkward.

"What are we doing today?" she asked.

He stood across from her in the kitchen, leaning on the counter. He wanted to pull her into him. He imagined her leaning her body against his, looking up at him. He would bend down and kiss her. Instead, he said, "I thought we would go to the Museum of Modern Art and then have lunch. Tom and Jessie are having friends over and we are invited. We'll leave at 6. Sound like a plan?"

"Yes it does, a good one."

Everything was perfect when they were together. They toured the museum, talking, laughing and always touching. Gray held her hand, or he had his arm around her waist. Carly would lean into him while they stood admiring a painting. He would move his arm up her back and rest his hand on her shoulder. Lunch was leisurely, they talked and spent time people watching before paying the tab and returning to Gray's apartment.

They had just enough time for a quick water before they left for the party. They got off the subway, stopped to pick up a six pack of beer, and went to Tom and Jessie's apartment. People were already there. Carly recognized the group from Friday night at the bar. Gray took her hand again, taking her with him to the kitchen. He pulled out two beers for them and put the rest in the fridge. He pulled the caps off the bottles and handed one to Carly. She took it from him, and he clinked his bottle against hers. "To the best week ever with my best friend."

"Here, here," she responded, taking a swig of beer.

He led her back into the living room where they circulated. Gray knew some of the other people there. They eventually got separated. Carly was having a fascinating conversation with a guy who had just returned from a six-week canoe trip up north in Canada, when she felt Gray's hand on her back. She leaned back against him. He removed his hand and circled her neck with his arm, his hand resting on her shoulder.

Luke joined the conversation. Gray bent his head to Carly's ear.

"Another beer?" he asked.

His breath was warm, it blew into her ear and down her neck. It was nice.

"Yes please," she breathed, looking into his eyes.

He returned her gaze. The walls, the people, the music, all faded away. It was just them. Carly's body pressed against him. Gray's arm around her, her body pressed against his.

A woman suddenly burst out laughing, breaking the spell. They both jolted with the reality of where they were. Gray jerked away from her. Carly straightened up.

"I'll get that beer for you," he said.

"Yeah, thanks."

Gray left for the kitchen, Carly headed for the bathroom. She was waiting in the hall for her turn, just outside the den.

"Wow, Gray and Carly look pretty serious," a woman said.

"Hardly. You know Gray," another replied.

"I've never seen him like this though. They both seem so happy."

"Yeah, she's a lucky girl," a third woman said.

"I asked him about her, sort of. I told him that they made a cute couple. He told me that they weren't a couple, they were just friends and when I told him he could have fooled me, he said he wasn't ready to settle down. That's why I don't think it's serious."

The bathroom door opened. It was Carly's turn. She scurried in, shutting the door behind her. What was that all about? They weren't a couple. She knew that. They were friends, best friends. She couldn't see them as anything else. Could she? No. No. Did Tap see her as more than a friend? No, he couldn't. Could he?

By the time she came out of the bathroom she was more confused about her and Tap than she had ever been. She walked back into the living room and spotted Gray. He saw her immediately and came toward her, beers in his hand. He handed her one.

"You know you're my best friend, right?" Carly asked.

"Yeah," he responded.

"And I'm your friend too," she said.

"My best friend, yeah." *Where is this going?* Tap wondered.

"Good."

At that moment Tom and Jessie joined them. The apartment was filling up as more people came. Carly was recognized and spent some time talking about her job and the other people on the show. She wandered away from that conversation and ran into Brett who had had a little too much to drink, but he was hilarious rambling on about this and that. Eventually one of Brett's friends came over and Carly left them to their discussion.

"Carly," she heard her name and looked up. Tap was standing in the hall, waving at her. She threaded her way through the crowd to him. He held out his hand and she took it. He pulled her to his side. "Having fun?" he asked.

She smiled up at him. "Most definitely."

A woman appeared in front of them. "Gray, darling" she exclaimed before kissing him on the lips.

"Nicole," he greeted her.

Nicole grabbed his arm and leaned against him. She looked at Carly. "And you are?"

"Katherine Parsons."

"Katherine, nice to meet you."

Tap interjected, "Nicole and I used to date."

"Oh, that Nicole, the one that made you resort to drinking a soda," Carly said.

Nicole looked at Carly again, then at Tap.

"Katherine is Gurl," Gray explained to Nicole.

"So you do exist! I have heard a lot about you."

"Likewise," Carly responded. "Mind you that was like three years ago, wasn't it?"

Suddenly there was an awkward pause as Carly and Nicole locked eyes. Carly knew all about Nicole and how manipulative she was. Carly didn't like her when she didn't know her, she liked her less now that she had met her.

Nicole broke eye contact and quickly said, "Oh, is that Tyrone?" Nicole looked over Carly's shoulder. She left them without another word.

Carly looked at Gray. "Your taste in women…"

"Yeah, you don't have to say anything else. But, my taste in friends." He grinned at her.

Carly held her beer up. "Hear, hear."

Gray tapped her bottle with his. "Amen."

CHAPTER FIFTEEN

Gray was at the gym. Carly was on the couch with her morning coffee when there was a knock on the door. She hesitated for a moment before getting up. She opened the door. A UPS man shoved a box at her. "Sign here," he said, holding out the UPS machine. She put the box under her arm, picked up the stylus and scribbled on the pad. He left and she put the package on the coffee table.

An hour later Gray came home, dropped his gym bag and went into the kitchen for a water. He plopped down beside Carly on the couch. She looked good in her t-shirt and shorts.

"You got a package," she said, pointing her mug at the coffee table.

Gray took another gulp of water, put down the bottle, picked up the package, pulled the tab and pulled out a binder. He looked at her and smiled.

"What?" Carly asked.

"Script," he responded.

They sat side by side on the couch. Gray read his part, a character named Buck. Carly read everyone else. They read until they reached a last scene between Buck and his broth, Don.

"I'm sorry Buck," Carly said.

"Yeah, you're sorry. Sorry like you were in Abilene," Gray responded.

Carly turned the page, looked at Gray and screamed, "fight!"

She jumped off the couch and took a swing at Gray. He dodged the blow. "What are you doing?"

She was bouncing up and down, her fists in front of her, "fight, fight, fight! What? You chicken? I'm ad libbing by the way. Bock, bock, bock." She threw another punch at him. All efforts to follow the script were thrown out the window.

Gray stood up then, imitating Carly's fighting posture. He threw a fist at her face, falling inches short. Her head rocked back. She came back with a punch to his gut, lightly connecting.

"Oof," he said as he sent out a jab, lightly connecting with her jaw. Again, her head flew back. She returned, one, two hits to the face.

Gray grabbed her in a bear hug. She lightly tapped his nose with her forehead and danced away. He put his hand to his nose. He pulled his hand away from his face and looked at the non-existent blood on his hand. "You broke my nose," he said, eyes twinkling.

"That's right. You deserve it!"

She followed that with another shot that tickled along his jaw.

He came back with an angel's brush to her face. She fell back on the couch, her eyes closed, her tongue hanging out of the side of her mouth. He held back a laugh.

He straddled her and patted her on the face. She lay still. "You knocked me out," she whispered.

He looked down at her, studying her face. He leaned forward and kissed her slowly, savoring her taste. Carly's eyes popped open.

She looked up at Gray. His eyes bored into hers. "Well now," he said. He leaned down and took her lips again.

She put her hand on his chest to stop him. Did she really want to do that? Stop him?

"You are not supposed to kiss Don," she whispered. "He's your brother."

"Sorry," he whispered. He leaned toward her again. She pushed harder against his chest and began to squirm under him.

"Besides," she continued, "I win this fight, Luke."

Gray hesitated for a moment. He needed to get his shit together. He straightened, leaned to one side and let Carly slide onto the floor.

Carly plopped down on the couch. She looked at her hands, examining her fingernails. Holy crap! That kiss came out of nowhere. She wanted more.

Gray stood there awkwardly. Carly was going to pretend that the kiss never happened. For the first time there was an uneasiness between them. He had caused this. He couldn't let his impetuous kiss ruin things between them.

He sat beside her, "I'm sorry."

"For what?"

"The kiss."

Carly turned toward him. "You should be sorry for that kiss."

"It won't happen again."

"I should hope not, because this is the way it's done." She straddled Gray and wrapped her arms around his neck. She looked at his lips, drawing closer. Gray moved to meet her. Their lips touched briefly. Carly pulled back, looked at him and smiled. "Well now yourself," she said before grabbing his shoulders and pulling him to her again. This time she claimed Gray's lips. She couldn't get enough of him. She pushed her body into his. She opened her mouth, inviting his tongue to enter. He pushed his tongue into her mouth, staking his claim.

They came up for air, breathing heavily. He smiled back at her, "Come here." He put his hands on her back and pulled her to him. He took her lips in a gentle kiss that deepened into something that wanted more. Gray leaned sideways, taking Carly with him. They lay on the couch, Gray pressing his body into the length of her while he ravaged her mouth.

He slid his hand under her butt, lifting her and pressing her into him. She could feel his erection through his shorts. She wanted it in her. She groaned from the want that was building in her. He pushed himself against her. She spread her legs. He pushed again, the friction from their clothing adding to their pleasure. He grabbed one of her legs and pulled it up while he pushed again and again. She was sopping wet, moving in time with his every thrust. My God she was going to come! He quickened his pace and began to grunt with each forceful thrust. She was coming, she had been holding her breath, waiting for this moment. The air rushed out of her lungs. Gray pushed one more time and collapsed on top of her, then rolled off her, onto the floor.

They stayed that way, in silence. Carly put her hand out and touched his cheek. He looked back at her and grinned sheepishly. "That was… surprising," he said.

"Very," she replied. She leaned toward him and kissed him gently.

He pulled her off the couch and onto his lap. He held her against his chest. She listened to his heart slow down.

"I need a shower," she said as she pushed away from him and stood. She looked down at him, put out her hand, and asked, "coming?"

He took her hand, stood and together they walked to the bathroom.

Carly took hold of his shirt, lifting it over his head. She leaned in to kiss his chest. She licked him and tasted the salty sweat of their lovemaking. He lowered his head, kissing her deeply while she slid his shorts over his hips and let them fall to the tiled floor.

He ended the kiss and pulled her t-shirt off. He unhooked her bra. She let it slide down her arms to join the other clothes on the floor. He palmed her firm breasts, so pale. Her nipples were pink and erect. She pushed her chest out, rubbing her nipples against the coarse hair on his chest. He pulled her in for another kiss, then undid the button on her shorts. Her shorts slid down her legs. She stepped out of them. She was wearing a thong. Gray ran his finger just under the elastic then pulled them down as well.

She was hairless. He put his hand on her mound,

rubbing the silky skin. He slid a finger in between her folds, feeling the moisture there. He kissed her again on the mouth, down to her chin, nuzzled her neck and then took a nipple in his mouth. He knelt before her, lifted one leg, put it over his shoulder, then placed both hands on her ass and licked the length of her slit. She moaned and put her hands on his shoulders. He leaned into her, probing her folds with his tongue. He pulled her forward, his tongue lapping at her opening. He found her pearl and sucked it into his mouth. He swirled his tongue around it making it harder. Carly ran her fingers through his hair, pushing him further into her.

Gray withdrew from her and stood. His erection rested against her belly. He leaned past her and turned on the water, adjusting the temperature. Together they stepped into the tub. They held each other, kissing passionately while warm water slid down their bodies.

"I'm going to fuck you, Gurl, don't go anywhere." He smiled as he stepped out of the tub, opened the medicine cabinet and pulled out a condom. He ripped it open and slid it over his length. Stepping back into the tub, he put his hands on her butt and lifted her against him, sliding her down and onto his erection. She gasped with delight as he filled her with his thick cock. She wrapped her arms and legs around him.

He pumped relentlessly into her. He couldn't stop, he couldn't get enough of her. His head was thrown back, the veins in his neck bulged. He felt her pussy tighten and begin to pulsate around him. She screamed her release. He thrust into her again and found his own relief.

Carly clung to him while her orgasm waned. She

released him and stood. Gray picked up the soap and lathered it in his hands. He ran his soapy hands over her body, down her shoulders, around her breasts, over her stomach and in between her legs. He knelt and washed her legs down to her feet. He turned her around and lathered her back, her buttocks and between her cheeks. She leaned back against him as the water beat down on her. His hands were all over her. She leaned her head back and he kissed her while he rinsed the soap from her shoulders, her breasts, her stomach and in between her legs again.

She stepped away from him. She felt his hands slide down her back and onto her buttocks.

He handed her the soap and she returned the favour, lathering his shoulders, chest, stomach and cock. She held him in her hand and reached down further to cup and squeeze his balls in her other hand. He reached out to grab her. She pushed him off and made him turn around. She reached up and lathered his shoulders, his back and his tight buttocks, sliding her hand in between them.

She rinsed the soap from his back. He turned around. He grabbed her and kissed her again.

They ran their hands over each other's bodies, rinsing off the soap. Gray turned off the water and they stepped out of the tub. He pulled a bath towel from a cupboard in the hall, and they took turns drying each other off.

Once dry, he took her hand and led her into his bedroom. He lifted the covers, and they slid in. Lying on his side he pulled her to him, wrapping his arm around her. They lay in silence until they fell asleep.

CHAPTER SIXTEEN

They woke in the late afternoon, warm and cozy under the covers. The phone rang. Gray got out of bed and went into the living room to take the call.

"Hey, man," he said as he walked back to the bedroom. "Nothing, just relaxing … hmm, let me check." He looked at Carly. "Roger, Brett, Patty and Luke are going out for pizza. Do you want to join them?"

Carly wanted to say no. She wanted to stay in bed with Gray. "Sure," she responded.

"Yeah. Where are you going? … Okay, when? … yeah, we'll see you there." He disconnected the call. "We've got about an hour to get dressed and get there."

Reluctantly Carly slid out of bed. She walked to the end of the bed, heading for the guest room and her clothes. Gray stepped in front of her. He put his hands on her shoulders and bent for a kiss. It was a quick peck, but it made her smile. Playfully she pushed him out of her path. "Later," she said.

"I'll be ready," he replied.

Gray was pulling on his briefs when his phone dinged—a text. He picked it up, read the message and smiled. It was Gurl.

Guerillagurl: Had a great time at your place, Tap.

Tapdat: Had a great time with you at my place, Gurl. When you coming over again?

Guerillagurl: I was thinking later tonight. You busy?

Tapdat: Busy with you Gurl. Can't wait.

Guerillagurl: Miss you already.

They walked hand in hand to the subway station. They stood together waiting for their train. Carly looked up at Gray. "Hey," she said. He looked down at her. Carly lifted her chin. Gray bent and kissed her. She returned the kiss, putting an arm around his neck. Gray deepened the kiss, putting both arms around her and lifting her against him.

"Man, get a room," someone said as they walked by.

Gray released her, letting her slide down his body. He reached into his pocket and pulled out his cell. He dialled a number. "Hi, it's Gray… yeah, something came up, Carly and I won't be able to make it," he said. "Maybe next time." He disconnected the call, took Carly's hand and together they hurried back to his apartment.

The door was barely closed before they were on each other, kissing and pulling at their clothes. They made it as far as the living room and the couch. Gray slammed into her until they came. Half dressed they sat up. Gray glanced at her. Carly's face was flushed, her hair sticking up. She looked at Gray. She smiled. Then she laughed. He started laughing too. He put his hands on her head and smoothed her hair down.

Gray pulled her onto his lap and pulled her t-shirt off before unsnapping her bra, freeing her breasts. He palmed one breast and pinched the nipple. Carly gasped. He moved her so that she was straddling him, her back against his chest. He took her other breast, giving it the same treatment. Carly squirmed with want. He released one breast and slid his hand over her belly into her slit, finding and rubbing her clit. She wanted him again.

He released her momentarily, grabbed a condom out of his jeans on the floor and put it on. He lifted her and slid his erection into her wet pussy before reclaiming her nipple and clit. He nuzzled her neck, breathing into her ear as he slowly made love to her while pinching her nipple and rubbing her clit. Carly and Gray slowly built toward another climax that was powerful when released.

Afterward, Gray lifted Carly and carried her into his bed.

Gray had gone to the gym by the time Carly woke. She grabbed one of his shirts, leaving it unbuttoned. Thinking of Gray, she daydreamed while she made her coffee. She cupped her breasts and tweaked her nipples before trailing her hand down her body, over her stomach to her pussy. She slipped a finger between her folds and rubbed her clit.

Her coffee was brewed. She picked up the hot cup cradling it in her hand. Leaning against the counter in the kitchen she held her mug looking out of the window, her mind replaying the day before. She could feel his hands on her breasts. Her nipples tightened. She could feel his tongue in her. Her juices began to flow. This was crazy! *Crazy good*, she thought. For years they had been best friends. Who knew they would end up as lovers? *Whatever*, Carly thought. It was fucking fantastic.

She heard his key in the lock. She put down her mug and walked to the door as he came in, closing it behind himself. He turned to drop his bag on the floor to find Carly waiting for him, the shirt she wore, his shirt, open, displaying her nakedness. She strode up to him, grabbed his head in her hands to pull his face down for a kiss while slamming his body backward against the closed door. Her kiss was demanding. She pressed her body against his and his cock come to attention. She dropped her hands from his face and pulled down his shorts. She fell to her knees and took all of him into her mouth. She slid him out of her mouth. She licked the tip of his cock and ran her tongue under his shaft.

He had his hands on her head, his fingers in her hair. He watched her slide him back into her mouth and began to suck, sliding him in and out at a furious pace. She held him with one hand. She put her other hand between her legs, roughly rubbing the nub that screamed for her attention. The sight of her sucking him and touching herself was heaven.

Gray braced himself against the door. Carly's mouth was wet and warm, demanding his response. He watched as his cock slid in and out of her mouth. He knew what she was doing with her other hand. He was so turned on he couldn't wait for her climax. He groaned and came in her mouth.

She released him and dropped her other hand to complete the job. Gray fell to his knees and took her lips, punishing her with a savage kiss. He took a nipple between his fingers, pinching and twisting it. She moaned into his mouth. He twisted her nipple harder and plunged his tongue into her mouth. She screamed and came, sagging against him. He held her as her climax wracked her body. He tightened his embrace and kissed her forehead.

"Good morning sunshine," he said huskily. What a woman!

They stood across from each other in the kitchen, Gray with his bottle of water, Carly with her mug of coffee. Carly was still wearing his shirt. It was still open. He couldn't not look at her, at her ivory breasts and pink nipples, at her naked mound.

She knew he was looking at her. She hopped up on the counter behind her, opening her legs.

"Why are you still dressed?" she asked.

"Good question," he responded, pulling off his t-shirt and stepping out of his shorts. "You drive me insane, you know."

"I know," she smiled wickedly. Her legs opened wider.

He stepped in between her thighs, putting both his hands on her ass and pulling her right up against him. "You will be the death of me."

She put her arms around his neck, breathing into his ear. "Fuck me first."

He retrieved a condom from his shorts and slid it over his erection. Then he pulled Carly off the counter. He turned her around, took his cock in his hand and guided it into her from behind. He pulled her up against him, his hands on her breasts as he pushed into her. She lifted her arms and linked her fingers behind his neck. He took her leisurely with slow strong strokes. He nuzzled her neck and stuck his tongue in her ear. She began to whimper. "Is that good?" he asked.

"Mmmm humm," she responded in a haze.

He squeezed her breasts. "Do you like that? Do you want me to stop?"

"No."

"No, you don't like that?" he asked releasing her breasts.

"No. Don't stop."

He took her breasts in his hands again, massaging them and palming her nipples. She whimpered again. He quickened his pace. He had no self control with her. He couldn't get enough of her. She drove him wild.

She brought her hands down to brace herself against the counter. She leaned forward and pushed her ass against him. He bent over her, ramming into her pussy, harder and harder. She was moaning now, urging him on, matching his every thrust. He gritted his teeth. He wanted her to come first or with him. He was almost there. He thrust into her. He felt her pussy tighten. She moaned. Once more and she would climax. He answered her unspoken demand and felt her pulse around him. He put his hands on her shoulders, thrusting into her one last time and exploding. He fell onto her, spent.

"I won't have to go to the gym if we keep this up," he panted.

"Am I being too rough on you, cuz you know I could stop," she teased.

"Don't you dare," he said as he slid his hand over her ass before giving it a light slap. "Don't even think about it."

They spent the last days of Carly's visit in his apartment, naked, enjoying each other and eating take out.

CHAPTER SEVENTEEN

Carly returned to L.A. on Sunday evening. Gray stayed in New York. He had rehearsals and costume fittings. She had to begin research on her next interview. They texted and Skyped to stay in touch. They missed being with each other.

A month later, Friday afternoon, Gray called Carly.

"Are you still at work?"" he asked.

"Yeah. I'm done though. I'm just shutting down. What are you doing?"

"Wasting time. That's why I thought I would call you. I couldn't think of a better way to spend a couple of minutes than talking to my Gurl."

"You're sweet. Who knew?"

"Shhh, it's our secret."

Carly slid her laptop into her case and threw it over her shoulder. She grabbed her purse and pulled out her keys. "I'm done now."

She pushed the elevator button. "I miss you," Gray said.

"Again?"

"Still."

The elevator dinged, the doors opened, Carly stepped in, and the doors slid shut. The call disconnected. Damn it! She would call him from her car. She rode down to the main floor, stepped out of the elevator, walked through the foyer and through the doors to find Gray leaning against the building, waiting for her. Her heart leapt and a smile lit up her face.

"Can I catch a ride with you?" he asked, smiling. God, she looked good.

"I don't know, where you headed?" she teased him.

"Wherever you're going."

"Then, of course you can."

He opened his arms. She walked into his embrace, leaning against him. He embraced her. It was just so right to have her in his arms. He had missed her, he knew that, but holding her against him now, he realized that she had become a part of him that he hadn't know was lacking. He kissed her forehead. When she looked up at him, he brushed his lips against hers.

"Let's go for dinner first," he suggested.

"Yes, let's. C'mon."

They got in her car and drove to a restaurant. They sat in a dimly lit corner across from each other. Gray took her hand in his and kissed her palm.

"What are you doing here, Tap?"

"Don't you want to see me?"

"Yes, I want to see you," she said. Gazing into his eyes she added, "more than that though I really want to feel you inside of me."

He felt his body react to her gaze and her words. If they hadn't just placed their order, he probably would have dragged her out of there and gone straight to her condo.

"I wanted to see you before I left. We're going to be shooting in Romania so I won't be able to see you for a while."

"In Romania? How long?"

"They're hoping to be done in three months."

"Three months!"

"Listen, can you get any time off? Maybe come for a couple of weeks or a few days now and then?"

"I can try but it doesn't look good. My line-up has been set for the next six months."

They sat in silence for a moment.

"What's three months in the scheme of things?" Carly said. "It's not like we won't see each other ever again right? We'll still text and Skype. I know it won't be the same as being together but it's better than nothing. Isn't it?"

"You're right. We're just going to have to cram three months of together time into this weekend."

"I know what I want to have crammed into me this weekend," she said slyly.

"Gurl, you're killing me."

"Eat fast," she said as the food was delivered to their table.

They barely made it into her condo. Gray closed the door and turned to take her into his arms. Carly kissed him with pent up passion, undoing his pants while he thrust his tongue into her mouth. She undid her skirt and pushed it down around her knees together with her panties.

Gray took her on the foyer floor, bracing himself on the palms of his hands, her ass sliding on the marble floor. Afterward they lay together. "Nice ceiling," Gray said.

She pushed herself up, stepping out of her panties and

skirt. She pulled her blouse up over her head and snapped off her bra. "You should see the bedroom," she said.

Gray was up in an instant, stepping on his pants and pulling them off. "I should, should I?" He took off his t-shirt, threw it on the floor and took a step toward her.

Carly screamed and ran for the bedroom, Gray in hot pursuit. He caught her just inside the door. He turned her toward him and lifted her into a kiss. He held her against him. She wrapped her legs around his waist, returning his kiss.

He walked with her to the bed and sat her on the edge. He kneeled in front of her. He spread her legs and put his mouth onto her mound, kissing the silky skin there. She wove her fingers into his hair. His tongue found the nub hidden in her folds. He sucked it into his mouth, twirling his tongue around it.

Carly sighed. She lay back on the bed, spreading her legs wider. Gray released her. He was hard again. He plunged into her and fucked her ferociously, grunting with each push, rocking the bed. She met each thrust. She could feel him deep inside of her. It still wasn't enough. "Harder," she panted. She was nearing climax, she needed more.

Gray pushed harder. "Is this what you want Gurl? You want this hard dick in your pussy?" he ground out as he plunged into her again.

"Yes, Tap. Yes. Fuck me harder," she moaned. She put her hands on her breasts, pinching her nipples.

Gray watched. He couldn't believe she could be any hotter or that his cock could get any harder. He pounded into her, he felt her tighten around his cock. He leaned forward and sucked hard on one of her nipples. She arched her back. He pushed again, coming deep inside of her. She spasmed and wrapped her arms around his neck. Moaning and hanging onto him.

Afterward Gray turned on his side to look at her. "You were right," he said. "The ceilings in here are even better than in the foyer." He leaned forward and kissed her gently.

They spent the evening curled up beside one another on the couch, sharing a bottle of wine. She told him about her next interview. He told her that Serena Scott would be playing the female role in the movie. Serena Scott, the most adored, sexiest woman in the film industry.

"I suddenly feel inadequate," she said.

"Inadequate! She's got nothing on you, Gurl," he exclaimed.

"How do you know that? You don't know that."

"What I do know is that she is not my best friend."

"You know she's single right?"

"Yeah, so are you. So what."

That stopped her. "Am I single?" she asked.

"Of course you are."

"Are you single?"

"Yes."

"So we, the two of us, are single." There was an edge to her voice.

"Yes. There seems to be something that I'm not getting. What are you trying to get me to say?"

"I'm not trying to get you to say anything. I just didn't

know I was single. I was thinking that I would miss you while you were in Romania but I just found out that I don't need to miss you. I can date someone else when I get lonely."

"Well yeah. Wait. What? No. You can't date while I'm in Romania."

"Why not?"

"Because I said so."

"And who are you again?"

"I'm the guy who makes love to you every chance I get. I'm the guy you dream about every night. I'm the guy that makes you need to change your underwear because I make you so wet."

"Oh. Then who am I?"

"You are the goddess who lets me make love to you every chance I get. You're the one I dream about every night. You're the one who makes me so hard I can't stand it."

"So, are we single?"

"No. We are not single. You, most definitely, are not single."

"That's better."

She was still annoyed, he could tell. He leaned over to kiss her. She put her hand in front of his face. Gray took her hand, kissed her palm and placed it on his cheek. He tried to kiss her again. She turned her face away.

He sat up straight, leaned over her and started gawking at the wall in front of her.

"What are you looking at?" she asked.

"I don't know. What are you looking at?"

"I'm not looking at anything."

"You must be looking at something because if you're not you are avoiding my luscious lips and hurting my feelings all at the same time."

She turned to look at him. He was grinning at her. "You are such a goof."

He leaned in and got the kiss he had been waiting for.

They ended the night on the balcony. Gray lay on the lounger, Carly astride him, making love slowly, gazing into each other's eyes and cut off from the rest of the world.

Gray and Carly joined her Saturday group for coffee at Coco's. After that they went to the farmers market and picked up ingredients for a candle lit supper. Gray cooked. Carly changed into a short flirty polka dot halter dress which plunged deeply in the front. They sat at the dining table across from each other. Gray served the appetizer, entrée and dessert.

They were finishing their wine when Carly leaned across the table and whispered to Gray. He stood, strolled around the table and pulled her chair out while she stood. He put his hand on her leg and slid it upward over her bare ass. He pushed her forward so that she was leaning on the table, and he flipped her skirt up. She was not wearing any panties.

He caressed her ass and slid his hand in between her legs. With his other hand he undid the tie of her halter, freeing her breasts. He took one breast in his hand while the other hand glided in and out of her legs.

Gray leaned over her, whispering in her ear. "Is that good baby? Do you like that."

Carly moaned. His hot breath in her ear and his hand rubbing between her legs made her want more. Much more.

"What do you want, Gurl? What can I give you?"

"I want you, Tap."

"But you have me."

Carly pushed herself down on his hand. He slid two fingers into her. She cried out in frustration. "I want more. I want your cock in me. I want you to fuck me. Fuck me, Tap," she demanded.

He released her breast and undid his pants. Freeing his erection, he pulled his fingers out of her, put on a condom and slowly slid his cock into her wet opening. Carly pounded her ass against him. "Is this better, baby?" he asked, teasing her with his cock.

"No. More, I want more." Carly started to ride his cock. Pushing her ass into his stomach, shoving his cock into her pussy and pulling forward, pulling him out and then shoving him back in.

Gray stood still as she worked his dick. He reached, grabbing her breasts, pinching her nipples. "Work for it, Gurl."

"Help me, Tap," she begged. She shoved her ass back into him, cramming his cock back inside. "Tap!" she screamed in frustration.

Gray released her breasts. He put one hand on the small of her back and pushed into her. He picked up his pace rocking her forwards and back. He reached down with his other hand and began to rub her clit. He threw his head back, ramming into her. He pushed into her again and looked at himself reflected in the windows of her apartment. He watched himself pound into her, saw her tits bounce with every push, the look of want on her face. Carly met his gaze in the glass, lowered her eyes and watched as he fucked her. Her pussy clenched around him. She moaned. "Tap," she said with desperation in her voice.

"I know," he said as he continued to push into her. He could feel her tightening around him. He was on the edge himself. "Hold on, Gurl, I'm coming for you," he told her as he picked up his pace. He put both hands on her hips, pulling her into him and pushing into her at the same time. Shoving in as deep as he could. Once, twice. He felt her tremble and then tense her body as a moan of satisfaction left her.

He was almost there. Her grabbed her nipple and squeezed. Carly screamed and clenched him even harder. He shot his load into her, hands on her hips again. "You are my heaven on Earth, Carly."

The next morning, they said their goodbyes in the condo. Gray held her for a long time, his chin resting on her head as he looked out the windows at the view of Los Angeles. Carly snuggled against him, listening to his heart beat. She always felt so safe in his arms.

The intercom buzzed. Gray's cab had arrived. He loosened his arms and looked down at Carly. He would miss seeing her eyes for the next three months, holding her, loving her. He bent his head and kissed her gently.

"I'm going to miss you so much," he said.

"Me too. We'll call and Skype as often as we can. Three months will fly by. I know they will."

He kissed her again and embraced her in a fierce hug. "I'll see you later, Gurl."

"You know you will."

He picked up his bag, opened the door and left.

CHAPTER EIGHTEEN

Carly was working late. She had an interview the next day and was doing a final edit of her questions. It had been a long day. She needed to take a break, take a step back. She picked up her phone and dialled Tap's number on skype. Tap picked up almost immediately. The phone caught his naked hip, just to the right of the money shot, his chest and finally his face as he sat down and faced the screen.

"Now this is the kinda call I like," she teased him.

He smiled at her. "I miss you."

"I miss you too. How's filming?"

"Tedious right now. Just waiting for confirmation we are done for the day."

"Guess what?"

"What?"

"I'm coming to see you. I've cleared a few days so I can spend some time with you."

He shifted his eyes to the left of the screen. "I'm not so sure that that's a great idea."

That was odd. Suddenly the whole tone of the conversation shifted to something uncomfortable. "Umm."

"It's just that I'm working long hours."

Carly felt something niggling at the back of her mind. "Where are you right now?"

"In my trailer."

Carly heard a door open in the background. He turned his head to the left. He looked back at the screen. "I need to tell you something," he said.

"Who are you talking to lover," a woman's voice asked him.

Carly's world skidded to a stop. She looked at Gray. He was watching her, watching the realization wash over her that he was naked in his room and there was a woman with him who had just called him "lover". She opened her mouth, then closed it.

Serena Scott leaned over Tap's shoulder and looked at her. Serena's shoulders were bare. Carly assumed she was probably naked too.

"Is this your little monkey girl, Gray?" Serena asked sweetly and then laughed.

"I wanted to tell you," he started.

"Tell me what? It looks like there's nothing to tell. I can see what's going on."

"We're friends, right? We never said we were anything else."

Carly didn't want to do this. She didn't want to hear anything more. She was sure there was a story, an explanation, an excuse, a fucking lie.

"You're right. We never said we were anything else. I just thought..."

"Thought what?"

"I just thought..." Carly turned her head to look behind her. There was no one there, but she said, "Oh, okay. Yeah, right away."

She turned back to face the screen. "They need me in editing. I've got to go." She disconnected without waiting for a response. She sat still, frozen, looking at her phone in her hand. It began to ring. It was Tap. She held her phone, waiting for it to stop ringing. It stopped. She put it down on her desk. It started ringing again. Tap was calling her again. She waited for it to stop ringing and when it did, she picked it up and turned it off.

She picked up her interview questions to finish her review. The pages started to tremble. She put them down. She would read them on her desk. Her vision blurred, she gasped, she didn't know what to do.

Should she stand up? Should she stay seated? Should she call someone? Should she go home? She just didn't know. She thought she should cry, but she couldn't. She wanted to scream, but she didn't. She stood up. She remained motionless, looking at nothing. When she finally did move it was to pick up her purse and her phone and leave.

She entered her condo, dumped her stuff, went into the kitchen and poured herself a glass of wine. She went to her bedroom and changed into her t-shirt and boxers. On the way out she picked up Bingo, her blue teddy bear. With Bingo under her arm and the wine glass in her hand she walked onto the patio and sat down. It was dusk. She took a sip of wine, watching the sky darken.

Were she and Tap ever anything more than just

friends? He had always introduced her as his friend, his best friend. So had she. They had never labelled their relationship as anything more than that. Were they friends with benefits? Yes. Were they more than that? She thought they were. She recalled the evening before he left for Romania when she had forced him to say that they were not single. He said that she was definitely not single. He never said anything about himself though. Maybe it was just her projecting her hopes and feelings onto Tap, assuming he felt the same way as she did.

Maybe the hard truth was that she was not enough for him, not enough to keep him interested, not enough to keep him faithful. Yeah, that hurt. Could it be true? Or could she just be sinking into the depths of despair wanting to hurt even more? She would go for option number two.

She started to replay the times they had spent together, rethinking everything that was said, rethinking every time that they had touched each other. Her throat hurt, and she had a pain in her chest. She picked up Bingo and looked into his happy, smiling face. "Oh, Bingo," she said before putting his soft round belly up to her face and finally breaking into tears.

She was in the makeup chair the next morning, waiting for Cali to apply her face. Cali came in, took one look at Carly's face and said, "Oh my God." She went to the mini fridge, pulled out an ice pack, wrapped it in a towel and approached Carly. She put the pack on Carly's cheek and held it there for a minute. She moved it to Carly's other cheek, then placed it on her forehead. She put it down, picked up eyedrops. "Look up," she instructed as she squirted drops into Carly's eyes. "See, you look better already," she said.

Carly looked at herself in the mirror. She still looked like shit. She looked as empty as she felt. She looked up at Cali.

"Nothing that some good make-up can't fix," Cali said, meeting her eyes in the mirror. "You're lucky I'm a professional." Cali tried a smile. Carly looked away.

Cali picked up a sponge and a jar and went to work applying foundation. "Whatever it is, it's going to be alright," she said soothingly. "Remember your first interview? You thought you were going to get fired and look what happened? Everything will work out okay."

The door burst open. A production assistant was standing in the door. "Cali, did you hear Gray North is dating Serena Scott?" Cali stopped what she was doing, meeting Carly's eyes.

Carly looked at the production assistant in the mirror who suddenly realized it was her sitting there. A look of panic crossed his face. Carly spun in her chair and threw her bottle of water at the closing door. The plastic bottle made contact and burst on impact, spraying water on the door and floor.

Carly turned her chair back toward the mirror. Cali applied rouge to a sable brush. She smoothed Carly's hair back. "You are going to live through this," she said as she lightly brushed Carly's cheekbone. A tear streaked down her cheek. "Now look what you did." Cali pulled a Kleenex from the box on the counter and began to dab at the tear. "Just remember, things could be worse." She dabbed at the next tear. "You didn't need that man anyway. How can you trust a guy like that? He's all over the world. He's never in one place for very long, all kinds of women throwing themselves at him."

"I know," Carly finally said.

"You know it, you feel it. I know it hurts. But this will pass." Cali picked up the sponge again, reapplying foundation where Carly's tears had streaked through it. She went back to the mini fridge and pulled out two tablespoons. She came back to Carly, placed a spoon in each of her hands and then picked up one hand and placed the underside of the bowl under Carly's eye. Carly applied the other spoon to her other eye.

A minute later Cali took the spoons from her hands. "Close them," she said. Carly closed her eyes while Cali applied eyeshadow. "Something better will come along," Cali said as he contoured Carly's eyebrows. "It always does. We always think there is nothing better, but there is. Whatever it is, it's just waiting for this moment to pass. Look up." Cali applied eyeliner and mascara.

Make-up done Cali and Carly looked at the results in the mirror. She looked perfect. "Sheila's gonna do your hair now," Cali said as she put her hands on Carly's shoulders. "You just have to make it through another two hours and then you're done." She squeezed Carly's shoulders. "You can do this. You are a professional. You got this."

Carly tried a smile, but it didn't work. "Thank you, Cali," she said. "I appreciate it."

Two and a half hours later Carly was done. She couldn't tell you how the interview went. If she hadn't been so well prepared, she couldn't have recalled the questions she asked.

She returned to makeup where Cali was waiting for her. She sat in the chair as Cali picked up a soft cloth and wet it with makeup remover. She began to softly wipe the makeup off Carly's face. "You did great. I knew you would. Now you're done. You can go home and take a long hot bath. Get that man out of your system."

She picked up another cloth and wiped Carly's face again. "Tomorrow is another day and all that crap, but you know what? It is." She squirted some moisturizer into her palm and with her fingertips she applied it to Carly's face. "Good as new," she said when she was done.

Carly left the office immediately. She walked out of the building wearing oversized dark sunglasses and came face to face with Janice, cameraman in tow.

"Katherine, did you know that Gray North was seeing Serena Scot?" she asked as she pushed a microphone into Carly's face.

"No. I just found out myself."

"How do you feel about that?"

"I imagine I feel just the same way you do, Janice. I hope they are both very happy."

Janice opened her mouth to ask another question.

"I'm late," Carly said. "Sorry, I don't have time for any more questions."

She walked briskly to her car as if she had an appointment to go to. Inside, her heart was compressed, barely beating. She had wanted to scream at Janice and tell her to fuck off and leave her alone. Instead, she started her car, picked up a dozen vanilla dipped donuts with sprinkles and drove home.

She walked into her condo, turned on the tv and picked up her first donut.

The intro for the celebrity gossip show played. *Gray North is spending time with Serena Scott in Romania*, the teaser blared.

Carly looked at the screen as a picture of Gray and Serena walking hand in hand appeared. She crammed the rest of the donut into her mouth. It was like a car accident on the side of the road, she couldn't look away.

Gray North and Serena Scot are getting cozy in Romania where they have been shooting the latest Carlos Garcea movie. A picture of Ken Curtis speaking to Gray came on. Gray had his arm around Serena's shoulder. She was resting her head on Gray's shoulder. *Reports are that Gray and Serena are spending every spare minute together.* They were sitting in a restaurant. Serena was laughing. Gray was smiling. *Serena divorced husband number three, the industrialist Kevin Freeland, while Gray was recently rumoured to be dating Katherine Parsons.*

Carly picked up another donut and took a huge bite. Her phone dinged. She picked it up. It was her dad. She put her cell down. She couldn't speak to anyone right now. Her phone continued to go off. It was her dad again, then Melissa, then Brittany, then her friends. Then Tap. She ignored them all.

She stopped after donut six. She picked up her phone and began to text her friends and family telling them she was okay but that she didn't want to speak to anyone right now. She would be in contact in the next couple of days. Then she deleted Tap from her contacts.

In a frenzy she logged on to her computer. She blocked Tap from her Facebook page. She deleted him from Messenger. She deleted him from Outlook. She called the doorman and told him to make a note that if Gray North ever came to see her, she was out.

CHAPTER NINETEEN

She took the next week off work. That was the week she had planned on being in Romania with Tap. Instead she stayed in her condo. She couldn't sleep and when she did, she more or less passed out from exhaustion. She deleted every text, email and message from Tap without reading or listening to them. By day five he stopped calling and texting.

When the next Saturday rolled around, she forced herself to shower, apply makeup and get dressed. She met her friends at Coco's. She sat listlessly as conversations flowed around her, barely taking part and briefly answering any questions thrown her way. When it was time to leave, she received hugs from one and all, and demands that she attend this function or that. She promised them all that she would. And she did.

She forced herself back to life again. She went to John's comedy set; a gallery showing with Terry and Greg; Josh's gig; and Stacey's slam performance. She went out for dinners, she went to movies, and she went shopping. It was hard work. She would have rather been at home with Bingo. But she did it.

When she was at home she worked. She started calling and texting her friends and family. She had to rehash everything with her mom and dad, Melissa and Brittany but it was cathartic. No more tears were shed over Gray North.

Saturday mornings were tough. No more morning chats with Tap. She avoided her computer. She would go for a run, stop for a coffee on the way home, or go to a park and watch other people living their lives.

The hard work started to pay off. Her feet were no longer coated in concrete. She could manage to stay awake and not feel listless. She even caught herself smiling at something on tv. She was getting over Tap but was she really? There was still such a huge hole in her life that she didn't know how to fill. Who could she call to talk about all the silly things in her life? Who else would understand the crises of her eating a donut and talk her down from a sugar overdose? She couldn't answer those questions because the only answer was Tap and he was no longer a viable answer for her.

A month later she received a telephone call from a respected televised national news magazine. One of their long-time correspondents was retiring and they were looking to fill his spot. Her name was on a very short list. Could she fly to New York for a meeting?

The meeting went well. She would continue to interview celebrities, only if she chose to, but she would also cover newsworthy topics, travel, sports, or anything of interest. She would have to pitch her ideas to the producer for approval and, if approved, the story was hers. She would not have to relocate but it would be better if she did. Was she interested?

She was at the airport, sitting in the front window of a

restaurant, killing the three hours before her flight home. She was happy. She had just ended the call where she was offered the job and she accepted it. She was emailing her dad, smiling, when she happened to look up.

Gray was coming home. He had been in Detroit visiting his family. He had been offered another movie and had some down time before shooting began. He was adrift. He seemed to have lost whatever it was that had been holding him in place and thought a trip home would help him find that anchor. But it didn't. He knew what it was though. He knew what was missing. He knew it was lost, that he was the cause of the loss, and that he would probably never get it back.

It was Gurl, his Gurl, his best friend, the woman he loved. Yes, he loved her. How could he not? She knew the real him, not the screen idol, and accepted him. He thought she had loved him too. When he had first met her, he had to keep touching her to make sure she was real, then because he just had to. He couldn't keep his hands off her. He wanted her so bad.

Everything about her made sense. Everything about them as a couple made sense. Everything about him when he was with her made sense.

He had ruined it. All by himself. He had no excuses. There was no explanation. He had missed Gurl. He physically yearned for her and there was no release. There was Serena though. She had thrown herself at him almost from the first moment they had met. It didn't matter to him that she was one of "The 10 Most Beautiful Women in the World" or "The Sexiest Woman Alive". There was nothing under those looks, no substance. She was no Gurl. But they were together all day long, every day, in a foreign land where he didn't know anyone else, and few people even spoke English. In a drunken moment of weakness, when he was hard and missing his Gurl, Serena had kissed him, and things just went from bad to worse.

He had hated himself for his infidelity. He knew that what he had done would end his relationship with Carly. He tried playing all scenarios where she would never learn about this affair, but none of them worked. He tried to figure out how to tell her in such a way that they would at least remain friends, but none of his calculations added up. He tried to imagine a way that he could tell her so that she wouldn't be hurt, but he knew it would destroy her.

So, like the coward he was, he continued his affair with Serena. The night Carly had Skyped him, he knew that that would be the end of them. He was hoping that it wouldn't, but he had watched her face when she realized what was happening, and he knew then that he had broken what they had had. In the annals of cowards, he was sure that he had won a prize of some sort. He had ended them quickly with no awkward explanation, almost like he had avoided the situation entirely.

She wouldn't answer his calls, she wouldn't return his messages or his emails. Why would she? Images and stories about him and Serena were all over the tabloids and the celebrity news shows. So, he had tried to make something with Serena, but he couldn't. Aside from the mediocre sex there was nothing between them. Once the movie wrapped, they split. The total debacle that ended his happiness with Gurl lasted a total of two and a half months.

He wanted to tell Gurl all about it. He wanted to talk to her about everything, like they used to, but he couldn't. He had lost such a big part of himself. When he had returned home, he was constantly reminded of her. He would see her all the time on the street or in the gym or some restaurant he was passing but when he stopped, he would realize it wasn't her.

And so here he was, in the airport, going home to an empty apartment, returning to his empty life. He was walking past one of those airport restaurants when he happened to glance in the window. He jerked to a stop, someone bumped into him, said something nasty and kept on walking.

It was Carly, the real Carly. She looked up, met his eyes and smiled. He gasped and smiled back. Was she glad to see him? Had she forgiven him?

When her smiled abruptly vanished and she avoided his eyes, he realized he had accidentally walked into her smile and that that smile had not been intended for him. He took a deep breath and entered the restaurant. He could not pass up this opportunity to speak to her, to plead his case.

Carly was so lost in her thoughts that it took her several seconds to realize that she was looking into someone's eyes. When she did, she mentally shook herself and then realized that it had been Tap that she had been smiling at. Oh my

God. Was he coming in? Of course he was. She felt like a deer in headlights, paralyzed at the sight of Tap smiling back at her, then walking into the restaurant. She wanted to get up and run out, but she couldn't, she was frozen. Even worse, what she really wanted to do was to run into his arms and cry into his chest about what had happened. She wanted him to soothe her and tell her it was all a mistake, a nightmare that was over. But she wouldn't do that.

He sat across from her and took her hand in his. When he touched her, she wanted to melt into him. But then she remembered the pictures of him and Serena. Her heart constricted painfully.

"Hey Gurl," he said.

She pulled her hand away. "Don't call me that," she said, looking at the table.

Tap sucked in a breath. That hurt. "How are you?"

"Good. I'm good."

"What are you doing here? This is like the last place I would expect to run into you." She was examining her fingernails. Then she looked out the window watching the travellers passing by.

Carly wanted to look at him, but she couldn't. "I've been offered a job here."

"Really!" He wanted her to look at him. She wouldn't. "Are you going to take it?"

"I don't know. I would have to move here. It's a big decision."

"Look at me Carly… please."

"I can't."

"It's still me."

"I know."

"Then why can't you look at me?"

Her gaze came back into the restaurant. Her eyes skimmed over the table between them, then to his chest. She took in a breath, and finally looked up into his eyes. "Because it hurts," she said as a tear rolled down her cheek.

His heart stopped. He could see the pain in her eyes. He could feel her pain in his heart.

The intercom blared, "Flight 514 to Albuquerque is now boarding at Gate 75."

"They're calling my flight," she lied as she shut her laptop, shoved it into her bag and stood. "It was great seeing you again, Gray."

"You don't have to go, Carly. You don't live in Aluquerque." He knew that she wanted to leave, that she was using the flight as an excuse.

"I know."

"Please," he begged. He reached for her again. She stepped away. He stood. "I'll walk you to your gate."

"Don't, okay?" she was begging him now. "Just don't."

"Please. You wouldn't talk to me. You wouldn't let me explain," he said.

"There was an explanation?" Carly's voice was acid. "A good explanation? Like it was an accident, right? She was dying and you had to give her naked mouth to mouth?" Carly's voice got louder with every word she spoke. "How stupid do you think I am?" She was practically screaming at him.

Gray knew he deserved all of her anger and he accepted it. "You're right. But you wouldn't talk to me. You wouldn't let me apologize. You wouldn't let me beg to come back. How could you just end us like that? After everything?"

"I think you did the ending, Mr. North," she spat his name.

"Oh my God, it is him. Gray North," a woman's excited voice came from behind Carly. She turned to find a young couple approaching them.

"Hey man, we are huge fans. Can we get a picture?" the man asked. "The folks at home are not going to believe this."

"Yeah, sure," Gray said as he watched Carly walk away. He took the man's cell and stood between the couple, her arm around his waist, his hand on Gray's shoulder. They smiled and he took the picture.

"Wow. Thank you so much," the woman gushed.

"It was my pleasure," he responded, smiling. He left the restaurant and ran to Gate 75, looking for Carly. She wasn't there. Of course she wouldn't be. She didn't live in Albuquerque. He checked the board. The flight to L.A. wasn't posted yet. It was a big airport, there were thousands of people there. She could be anywhere. He left, regret heavy on his shoulders.

CHAPTER TWENTY

Carly had accepted the job in New York, but not without some trepidation. She knew that she would be living in the same city as Gray and that there was the chance, however slim, that she would run into him again. But it was also about leaving the life that she led here, the friends that she had and the community they had built. It was the opportunity that had made up her mind, the opportunity to move from celebrity interviews into serious journalism.

The show was on summer hiatus. She would have six weeks to sell her condo, wrap up her life in L.A., and find a place to live in New York. There were a lot of things to get done in a short period of time.

Her besties, Melissa and Brittany, came for a week to say goodbye to the condo and L.A. They spent their time reminiscing about the past and their exploits in L.A., they shopped, they went to functions with Carly's friends. The one thing they did not do was talk about Gray.

Until the night before the girls would return home.

They were on the balcony, drinking wine. "You know I ran into Gray at the airport when I was in New York," Carly said.

Melissa and Brittany looked at each other.

"Why didn't you tell us?" Melissa asked. She had always

been the most courageous of the three, willing to meet any problem head on.

"I wasn't ready to tell anybody," Carly replied.

"Well," Brittany said. "What happened? Did you speak to him? What did you say?" Her voice was soft with compassion.

"Not much. We spoke for a minute or two."

"And…" Melissa pressed. Carly knew there was no distracting her now that she knew about Gray.

"And nothing. I ran away at the first opportunity."

"Really? That's all," Brittany said sarcastically. "Do you still have feelings for him, even after what he did?"

"No. I don't still have feelings for him." The words felt wrong the moment they left her mouth. Her heart painfully contracted. She had to stop denying her true feelings if she expected to move forward. "I still love him. I miss him every day. I miss everything about him." She was crying for God's sake. She thought she was done crying over him.

Brittany went to her and hugged her. "Can you forgive him, Carly?"

"I could. I want to. But then what? What about the next time he's on location and I'm not with him? How many times would I have to forgive him? How many broken hearts can I live through? I can't live like that. I don't want to live like that."

"You know, I always thought he just panicked," Melissa said.

Brittany and Carly looked at her.

"You know," Melissa continued, "some guys panic when they finally realize that they've found the woman they love. I don't why or how that reasoning works, but they panic. It's like they suddenly realize this is it, they want to make the big commitment but they're scared. They panic. The screw around with whatever is on hand. They know they fucked up but it's like they can't help themselves. I think Gray panicked."

"That doesn't make sense," Brittany said.

"I know it doesn't make sense but I can name three couples I know where that happened," Melissa responded.

"What happened to those three couples?" Carly asked.

"Two of them got back together. They're still together, still happy. I think Gray panicked, Carly. I think you should give him another chance."

"I can't take that chance," Carly replied. "I'm starting a new job. I can't be an emotional mess. What if he doesn't want to…" She mimicked quotes with her fingers. "'Get back together'? I don't know if I could be happy with anything less. Being his friend again wouldn't be the same. I would always remember what we could be. I would always want that."

They sat in silence, drinking their wine, considering the conversation. Finally, Melissa said, "I still think Gray panicked. But you have to think of yourself in this situation. You have to make yourself happy."

"That's right, Carly. You have to think of yourself," Brittany said. "Whether you take him back or not. It's your decision. I love you and I will support whatever decision you make."

"That's right," Melissa added.

They finished the bottle of wine and went to bed. The girls had to be up early to catch their flight.

Carly drove them to the airport. They parted with hugs and promises to meet in New York once Carly was settled. Carly thought that what Melissa had said last night made sense, but she didn't know if it was true in Tap's case. Maybe she just wanted it to be true. What if it was true? Would she take him back? Would she be brave enough to trust Tap with her heart again?

The week after that her mom and dad drove in to help with the heavy lifting.

It was the Saturday before her last week in L.A. She was at Coco's with the group. Stacey asked them all to come to a slam night on Thursday. She would be performing, but it would be open mic night. These nights were sometimes surprising and fun. They all knew how important it was to receive support and appreciation from strangers.

Carly said she would go on one condition. They would all meet at her condo for dinner first. She had a ton of food she had to get rid of. She wasn't promising a gourmet dinner, it would be a mish mash of this and that, but she wanted them there. Plus, there was liquor that she didn't want to have to transport to New York. That was when they all agreed to attend.

Thursday came around much too fast. Carly had lined up showings with a real estate agent in New York; she had set a date and time for the movers to come get her stuff, and had confirmed her flight to New York. That was just in the morning.

She spent the afternoon cooking. When everyone arrived there was soup, salad, macaroni and cheese, baked chicken, some pork skewers, rice, vegetables, cheese, crackers, and of course, wine and cocktails.

By the time they got their cabs and made it to the club they were noisy and boisterous. By the time the poetry started they were winding down and ready for the performances. Stacey was toward the end of the show. She had fans in the audience as well as her friends. She got up and performed her poem. She waited for the applause and cheers to die down.

"I've been mentoring someone for the past couple of weeks. He's here tonight. You guys are a great crowd and you know that us insecure artistic types need all the adoration we can get. So, please, give a big welcome to my student."

The crowd cheered and applauded. Stacey ran off the stage and back to the table where she sat beside Carly. She leaned over and shouted into Carly's ear, "You promised you would stay, Carly! You promised you would listen!"

Carly thought that that was odd. Why wouldn't she stay? She did promise. She nodded her head at Stacey. Meanwhile the crowd went nuts. Women were screaming, someone was whistling. She looked toward the stage. Gray was standing in front of the microphone.

The world just stopped. There was no sound, no air. Carly was in a vacuum. There was just her sitting at the table and Gray on the podium in front of her. The breath that she was holding suddenly rushed out of her lungs and she inhaled deeply. The room filled with people and noise again. She reached for her purse to leave. Stacey grabbed her arm.

"You promised to stay," she reminded Carly.

Gray was smiling and nodding his head. He held up his hands, motioning people to quiet down. Several seconds later the cheering and clapping had stopped.

Carly was transfixed. She gobbled up the sight of him, his hair, his eyes, his mouth, his chest, his hips, everything. She was torn. She wanted to jump up and leave and run up onto the stage and throw herself at him. She missed him so much. She missed talking to him, laughing with him, making love to him.

Gray, leaned toward the microphone. He opened his mouth and began to speak. "I recently lost a good friend of mine. My best friend. This is dedicated to her."

There was silence in the club.

"I was the fool, there is no one else to blame
I was caught unaware by the emotions that came
With her. She who was so perfect in every way
Her hair, her eyes, her lips, her soul, even the air
     surrounding her affected me in a way
That I had never felt before. She looked at me and I
     could see the man I wanted to be.
Her voice, her smile, her touch, her presence all made
     my life worth living.
She was the reason the word perfect was first spoken

She was the reason my sun rose in the morning
And yet I took her love and used it as a token
To be spent on something shiny and new
As if something more perfect than perfect existed"

"You dog!" a woman in the crowd shouted at Gray. Other women in the crowd voiced their agreement. Gray acknowledged them with a nod.

"I was the fool, there is no one else to blame
No explanation, no justification, no clarification
You deleted me from Facebook, you blocked me on
    Messenger
You refused to answer my calls, you didn't respond to
    my emails
I held my hand above the water, waiting for you to take
    it and pull me out
You abandoned me when I needed you the most
To help me make sense of what I had done, to forgive
    me the for the monumental
Mess that I had made of us
To let me fill my lungs with the sacred air that was you"

"You deserved it baby!" a woman shouted. Other people clapped their agreement. Again, Gray acknowledged them with a nod.

"I was the fool with no one else to blame
You left me broken, set adrift on the sea

No home, no harbour, no shallows to protect me from
    the sea of guilt and shame
I bathe in every day
I cling to memory of you in the hope that you will relent
That you will give me a sign that maybe we are not
    done forever
That your icy resolve will melt a tiny drop of water
That your desert will release a single grain of sand
That your heart will open a hairline crack
To let me back in"

"The man's sorry!" the guy at the next table shouted. "Give him another chance!" someone else yelled.

Gray found Carly in the crowd. His eyes met hers and he continued. He took the mic off the stand. He left the stage and threaded his way through the crowd.

Carly was glued to her seat. Gray was coming toward her. He was speaking to her and what he was saying was important, but she couldn't make sense of the words. She couldn't hear them over the sound of her heart beating in her chest.

Gray could tell that Carly was torn. He sensed that if given the opportunity she would bolt. But Stacey was holding her hand. Keeping her at the table. Then he stood in front of her, his eyes boring into hers.

"I was the fool with no one else to blame
But you can't delete you
Your scent is in my air
You can't delete you

You are in my blood, in my marrow and in my bone
You can't delete you
You are in my thoughts and in my dreams
You can't delete you
You are in my soul and in my heart
You can't delete you
You are in my memory and in my DNA
You can't delete you
You are why I still have hope
You can't delete you"

He stopped speaking. There was silence for a moment and then the club burst into applause and cheers. Carly couldn't move. She was still processing the words that he had said to her. He squatted in front of her, watching her face, trying to read her thoughts.

He reached out and put his hand on hers. She looked at his hand. Her gaze travelled up his arm to his face, his eyes. She stood. He stood with her. She was so rigid.

"Please, Gurl," he said.

Carly pulled her hand out of his grasp, picked up her bag and left the club. She pushed through the doors into the fresh air. She stood still gulping in the cool air, fighting the tears that threatened to spill out of her eyes. She turned toward the parking lot and began walking to her car.

Behind her she heard the club doors bang open, then feet pounding the pavement, coming toward her. Then Gray stood in front of her, blocking her. He was angry.

"Talk to me," he demanded. "I made such a huge mistake, I know that. What I didn't know was that you were more than my best friend. You were the one and only girl I ever loved. I've loved you since we fought the rats in the sewer system when we were twelve. Please, Gurl."

"You really hurt me, Tap. How can I ever trust you again? What about the next time you have to shoot on location and we can't be together for months at a time? I can't live a life like that. Maybe it's best that we…"

"Don't say whatever it is that you were going to say, Gurl," he pleaded. "I need you in my life. I won't make that mistake again. I've learned a hard lesson. I have never been as lost and alone as I have these pasts months without you. I can't let you go. I don't make sense without you. Please."

He could tell she was fighting with herself. He could see her resolve strengthen then waver. He put one hand on her shoulder. She didn't shrug it off. He put his hand on her other shoulder and pulled her toward him. She resisted, standing her ground. Suddenly she relaxed. He pulled her again. She walked into his arms. He folded her into his embrace. He released the breath that he had been holding.

"I don't know what to do, Tap," she confided in him. "I need you. I need you to talk this through with me and tell me that taking you back is the right thing to do because that is what I want to do. Can you be my best friend again for the next five minutes?"

"Of course, Gurl," he choked on the words. "I would do anything for you. You know that. As your best friend, I have to tell you that I always liked Tap. I thought he really cared for you and always had your best interests at heart. No one is perfect, Gurl. He made a big mistake with your heart and he is so, so sorry, he told me that himself."

"I know he's sorry, Tap, but that really hurt. I can't do that again. I don't understand why it happened in the first place. Maybe I'm not woman enough for him. Maybe that's why."

He pulled her away from him and shook her by the shoulders, then bent down to look her in the eyes.

"That is not it, Gurl," he ground out, "you are woman enough for him. You are the only woman for him. Don't you ever think that what happened was your fault in any way."

Carly sobbed and fled back to the safety of his arms.

"Why, Tap? Why did you do it?"

"I was drunk, I missed you so very much, Serena was constantly on me. But I don't want to make excuses. Someone once said to me 'it's just another in a long line of things I don't know.' I have hated myself every day because of it. I would never do it again. I love you so much, Gurl. So does Tap. It would not be a mistake for you to take him back. Give him one last chance, Gurl. Please."

She looked up at him.

"Hey," she said.

He looked down. She raised her chin an inch. He bent his head and claimed her lips.

The next day, they got out of a cab and put their luggage on a cart. Gray took Carly's hand in his and turned toward the airport doors to come face to face with Janice, her cameraman in tow.

"Gray, are you and Katherine back together again?" She asked.

Gray looked at Carly and smiled. "We are."

"So she's forgiven you?"

"Janice, that's kind of none of your business but yes, she has forgiven me. I am man enough to admit to the huge mistake I made and she is wonderful enough to forgive me."

"Where are you two headed?"

"To New York. Katherine is moving there for a new job."

"Moving in with you?"

"Janice, I am going to miss you. My response to your last question is that yes, she is moving in with me and there are nothing but great things ahead for both of us. That's the plan anyway."

"Thanks Gray, best wishes for the both of you." She turned to the cameraman. "Cut." She turned back to Gray and Carly. "I was rooting for you two."

They left Janice on the sidewalk looking for her next celebrity encounter.

They sat in the boarding area for an hour. Tap responded to emails while Carly read an article on her laptop. When their flight was called Tap stood up and stretched before putting his hand out to Carly. "You ready?"

"Locked and loaded, Tap."

He pulled her out of her seat and into his arms.

"Let's go," he said as he gave her a quick hug.

"Balls to the wall!"

EPILOGUE

Shooting was over for the day. Tap walked into the house he had rented for himself in Winnipeg. It was a quiet tree lined street of stately homes. The summer sun was fading, the temperature falling ever so slightly.

He missed Gurl. He was going to call her in about ten minutes if she wasn't at home. He needed to at least hear her voice.

He went to the bedroom and stripped. It had been a hot day. He was sweaty and needed a shower. He opened the door to the en suite and stopped.

She was already there, sitting in the double glassed in shower, naked, waiting for him. She looked at him and smiled that wicked smile. She leaned back on her hands pushing her breasts forward for his eyes only. His groin tightened. She stood and turned on the water. He admired her as the drops slid down her body, over her shoulders, her ivory breasts and pink nipples, and down her belly, dripping from her hairless mound. She smiled at him again, cupping her breasts and then trailing one hand down her chest over her stomach and between her legs. She rubbed against her hand, watching him.

Carly had put in a full day's work. She had had Zoom

meetings, conducted telephone interviews, reviewed her emails and sent out a few more. She would do a first draft of her story tomorrow and then draft a shooting schedule to obtain footage to flesh out her story. She hadn't heard from Tap all day. She knew he had had a full day of filming.

She had just stepped into the shower when she heard him come in. She sat and waited for him to undress. When he walked into the en suite naked she felt that tug in her stomach whenever she saw him. She turned on the water and gloried in the way he looked at her. She could see his cock stiffen. He watched as she teased him. He grabbed his erection and slid his hand up and down his cock several times. She felt her body respond. Her nipples tightened. Her juices began to flow.

Tap picked up a bar of soap and grinned devilishly at her. Carly laughed. He pulled opened the shower door and joined Carly under the water. He pulled her into his arms, kissing her deeply. He let her go and lathered up the soap in his hands. He put them on her breasts, palming her nipples and slowly circling her breasts with his soapy hands. He slid his hands down her stomach to her mound. Carly moved her leg. Gray slid his hand between her legs. Carly moaned and grabbed his shoulders, leaning into him. He put his hands on her ass and lifted her, sliding her down his chest and onto his cock. Carly sighed.

This was the way it was supposed to be. She was supposed to be with him. He was supposed to be with her. They were supposed to be together. Always.

About Geneva Gordon

Geneva is a hardy Canadian who shares her home with her cat, her son, and the birds and squirrels that she feeds in her backyard. She is an avid reader who has read all genres of fiction and the odd non-fiction book as well. Romance novels are her favorite and she strives to make her readers get involved with her characters: to feel the giddiness of discovery, the tension of desire, to smile, to get that feeling in the pit of your stomach when things don't go well, and to rejoice when the lovers find their way back to each other. She looks forward to sharing her stories with you.

Books by Geneva Gordon
One Task: The Warrior and The King
You Can't Delete You

Also from Deep Desires Press!

The Frozen Prince
Minna Louche

Genevieve is a mere servant girl for the royal family, who's best friend happens to be the princess, Malaya. When a powerful and dangerous man attacks the castle in an effort to steal the princess, Genevieve acts quickly to save Malaya—by offering herself instead.

The thwarted abductor, however, is no ordinary man. He is the Frozen Prince—a supposed urban legend cursed with an ice-filled heart and dark magic. When Genevieve is swept away to his isolated castle in the Northern Mountain, however, she discovers that there is far more to the legend than has been told. Like the unimaginable depths his ethereal white eyes hold...and the hold they have on her.

Genevieve is trapped between something sinister hiding on the mountain and a cursed prince whose carnal cravings gnaw at his heart. Emblazoned in the icy clutches of desire, if they can't solve the mystery behind the Frozen Prince, neither will survive.

Available in ebook and paperback!

Also from Deep Desires Press

Silk & Swords
Christopher Stires

An alluring young woman damned with a curse challenges the heartless assassin commanded to kill her.

A bereft widow discovers the delights of the marriage bed with a ferocious knight-soldier.

A sensuous female barbarian and her ardent diplomat husband investigate the mysterious murder of a masked prisoner.

Three entwined tales of love and eroticism…tales woven together for the titillation of a powerful, meddling, yet well-meaning queen by a wise, unsettling, sooth-saying oracle.

Plunge into a world where desire and lust rule peasants and royalty alike. Enter the passionate world of Thuria.

Available in ebook and paperback!

Misled by a Monster
Marco May

Mitch has never quite fit in. He's always felt...different somehow, though he could never put his finger on it. When he meets Stan, a strange and mysterious man, he feels an instant attraction and like someone finally truly understands him.

The allure of Stan is so powerful and all-consuming that Mitch soon packs up and leaves everyone behind to move in with Mitch in his rural community. But once ensconced there and separated from everything he used to know, Stan changes. And Mitch is trapped. And there are strange things going on around him...otherworldly things.

Stan's twin brother Wes seems to be Mitch's only hope of escape—and of love. For where Stan is evil, Wes is good. Will Mitch be stuck in misery with Stan? Or is there hope for him and happiness with Wes?

The secrets soon spill and the truth comes out. And the most shocking revelation of all for Mitch? He might not be quite human himself.

Available now in ebook and paperback!